MILLY AND THE TOMB OF
ALEXANDER

BY

J P ALLEN

DEDICATION

To Louie Roi for being an inspiration to us all.

J P Allen

ACKNOWLEDGMENT

Thank you to my wife, my children and my dog for being there when I needed you.

TABLE OF CONTENTS

PRELUDE

In the heart of Punjab, India, where the Hydaspes River slithered like a giant serpent through the mountains and nearby villages, Alexander and his brave Macedonian army stood face-to-face with their greatest opponent yet. On the opposite side of the riverbank stood Porus, a proud Indian king. Although Porus knew the battle would be bloody, he was determined to defend his land against Alexander the Great and his forces. As the sun illuminated the battlefield, Alexander pondered his next move. He knew that a direct attack on Porus's stronghold would be a recipe for disaster. Yet, Alexander was no stranger to challenges, in fact, he thrived on them. With cunning and guile, he hatched a daring plan to outsmart King Porus.

His eyes scanned the river's edge for any sign of opportunity. Night after night, accompanied by his hoplites, he crept along the shore, searching for a way to cross. Finally, he found an uninhabited, wood-covered island upstream from his camp. Smiling to himself, Alexander gathered his cavalrymen around him and revealed his plan. "We'll cross here," he said. "And attack the Indian cavalry from the right. They'll never see it coming."

Meanwhile, Porus kept a watchful eye from the southern bank, unaware of the danger lurking in the shadows. His scouts patrolled diligently, but they were blind to Alexander's clever ploy. As dawn broke, the Macedonian army burst forth from the mist, their banners fluttering in the breeze. With a mighty roar, they surged towards Porus's camp, catching the enemy completely off guard.

The clash of weapons reverberated across the battlefield, and Indian elephants, majestic and fearsome, charged into battle, , their trumpets echoing like thunder. However, even these mighty beasts could not withstand the relentless assault of Alexander's troops. With each passing moment, the tide turned in favour of the Macedonians. Alexander himself led the charge, his sword flashing in the sunlight as he carved a path through the enemy ranks. It was a blur of blood, sweat, and mud, and Alexander, with adrenaline coursing through his veins, couldn't help but let out a fierce battle cry as he took down Indian cavalrymen and war elephants left and right.

Yet, amidst the chaos, one figure stood tall, King Porus, mounted atop his war elephant, fought with a fire in his belly. Despite his bravery, Porus could not stop the advance of Alexander's army. With his forces scattered and his kingdom in disarray, defeat seemed inevitable. Still, he fought on, determined to defend his land, no matter what. As the dust settled and the echoes of battle faded, it became all too clear to Porus that he had lost. Alexander approached him with respect and admiration. When Alexander asked how he wished to be treated, Porus simply replied, "Treat me as a king would treat another king." Alexander was impressed and allowed King Porus to retain his lands.

The next day, Alexander rode back to Babylon, where he had established his seat of power. The city greeted him with adoration and celebrated his victory from dawn until dusk. For Alexander, the spoils of victory were bittersweet. His body, once invincible on the battlefield, had begun to betray him. A mysterious illness had taken hold, quickly sapping him of his strength and clouding his mind. As time went by, Alexander lay bedridden, haunted by his mortality. Less than two years ago, he had conquered King Porus's army. What would that brave king think if he could see me now? he thought to himself.

Alexander's loyal friend, Sisygambis, who he saw as a mother figure, never left his bedside during this time. Clutching his hand, she asked him, "What shall I do, dear Alexander? What shall I do when the time comes for you to pass on?"

Alexander managed a weak smile. "You must find a place for me to rest in Alexandria, mother," he said. "Protect my riches and uphold my legacy, no matter what it takes." A few minutes later, he passed away in her arms. Sisygambis, the birth mother of Darius III, with tears streaming down her face, closed her eyes and prayed to the gods and goddesses for guidance. She understood that Alexander had bestowed upon her a solemn and sacred duty. "Mighty Athena... bright Apollo..." she said, her voice trembling. "Give me the strength I need to conquer this challenge and do right by my adopted son, Alexander."

She strapped Alexander's riches and his body to her horses and set out on a mission to find the perfect resting place for her son. She knew that the royal cemetery would not do. If Alexander's grave were out in the open, it would no doubt attract vandals and thieves. Although Alexander had been well-liked by the Alexandrians, he was not immune to the envy of street urchins, travelling merchants, and royal subjects alike. Sisygambis had heard whispered legends of tunnels beneath the streets of Alexandria, which served as secret passages for those who had resided in the city before it surrendered to Alexander the Great. She found a secluded spot behind the palace and began to dig.

After traversing the winding tunnels, her back aching from carrying Alexander's immense wealth, Sisygambis discovered a site of ancient significance, a burial chamber fit for a king. Ecstatic, she returned to her horses to retrieve Alexander's body. With the help of a trusted royal subject, she laid Alexander to rest, surrounded by the riches befitting a conqueror of nations. Sisygambis knew, however, that to truly protect her son's legacy, she would need to conceal the tomb from those who would seek to steal Alexander's riches. She devised a series of traps and illusions to protect the entrance, ensuring that only the worthy would be able to find their way to Alexander's final resting place. And so, for many years, the great conqueror slumbered, his secrets hidden from the world, that is, until a young girl and her very clever dog went in search of the entrance to Alexander's mysterious tomb while the streets of Alexandria were being stormed.

1

THE CITY'S SECRET

Captain Catalina, Mirabel, Wolfstan, and Faramund raced through the narrow, winding streets of Alexandria, their armour clanking with every hurried step they took. The once-bustling city, which had been a vibrant hub of culture and commerce, was now crumbling around them, engulfed in chaos and despair. Villagers huddled in their mud-brick homes, trembling in fear as the echoes of turmoil reverberated through the air. It was abundantly clear that the news of the caliph's death had spread like wildfire, and with his passing, any semblance of security within the city had vanished into thin air. For Captain Catalina and her companions, however, this was good news. Their king had tasked them with retrieving a rumoured treasure, and now, with the city in disarray, it lay ripe for the taking.

"Another successful raid!" Faramund declared triumphantly, raising his sword to the sky with unrestrained glee. "Where do you think the caliph kept his riches?" His enthusiasm was palpable, and it was infectious, but Catalina knew they had to remain cautious.

"Keep your voice down, Faramund," Catalina hissed, motioning for them to be quiet as they approached one of the caliph's grand palaces. "We don't want to attract attention." The entrance was heavily guarded, and she knew all too well that the caliph's soldiers would , defend his wealth to the death. The chaos of the raid had already scattered their fellow crusaders, leaving them severely outnumbered and at a distinct disadvantage.

"Shall I deal with the guards, Captain?" Wolfstan asked, nocking an arrow onto his bow with a practiced ease. Stocky and muscular, Wolfstan was no stranger to battle. Despite being the lone Frenchman among them, , his skills with a bow were unparalleled. "My wife's sleep arrows are potent. I told her, 'We're only aiming to put them to sleep for an hour, darling.'" He aimed at one of the guards, a glint of mischief in his eyes. "Oh well, "

"Hold on," Catalina interrupted, grabbing his arm firmly. "There are too many of them. We need to find another way in." She beckoned for the others to follow and began to sneak along the palace wall, her keen eyes scanning for a window or any weak spot, , anything that would grant them entry without being noticed. After some time, they found themselves in the palace's courtyard. To Catalina's dismay, it had already been ransacked. The stables were empty, and the marble pillars that had once lined the garden now lay shattered on the ground, remnants of a once-grand estate.

She scanned the outer wall for a back entrance but saw nothing promising. "What are we supposed to do now?" she muttered, frustration creeping into her voice. "We can't return to King Jason empty-handed, "

Just then, Mirabel's sharp eyes caught something unusual beneath a fallen pillar. She gently touched Catalina on the shoulder and pointed it out. "Look there, Captain," she whispered, her voice barely above a breath. "What's that?"

The two of them crouched down, and with some effort, aided by Wolfstan and Faramund, they rolled the massive pillar , aside. Beneath it was a small wooden door, almost hidden from view, covering what appeared to be an entrance to an underground passage.

"Good eyes, Mirabel!" Catalina exclaimed, her face lighting up with excitement. She reached down to open the door, but as soon as her fingers brushed against it, she gasped and jerked her hand away. "It burns!" she cried, her voice laced with shock. "Why does it burn?"

Before anyone could react, Faramund, thinking it was an ordinary door, swung his sword at it with all his might. The blade struck the wood with a violent crack, and he was thrown several feet back, landing hard on the ground. He lay there for a moment, gasping for breath, before finally sitting up, a look of bewilderment on his face. "That's no ordinary door," he said, rubbing his chest as he tried to regain his composure. "It's protected by the gods!"

The others looked at him, perplexed by his sudden revelation.

"What do you mean?" Wolfstan asked, his brow furrowed in confusion.

"It's enchanted," Faramund said, standing up and running a hand through his long hair, his expression serious. "The gods and goddesses are on the caliph's side, it seems."

"Of course," Catalina muttered, rolling her eyes in exasperation. "But we still need to find a way inside. This could very well be the entrance to the secret chamber. There could be treasure beyond our wildest dreams down there, "

"Milly! Come down for breakfast!"

The palace courtyard instantly dissolved into pixels, and the four knights, , now mere avatars on Milly's computer screen, , stood around the mysterious wooden door, unsure of what to do next.

"Sorry, guys," Milly said into her headset, her voice tinged with regret, "Mum's calling me." She sighed, knowing her mother had promised to explain how she ended up trapped in Athena's Shawl in the first place. Milly had been waiting for answers, her curiosity piqued.

She glanced at the mysterious white cloth hanging in her window. The characters from War of the Ages 2 danced across the fabric in the sunlight, like shadow puppets brought to life. Milly smiled, recalling that if she touched Athena's Shawl while the game was projected onto it, she'd be transported back to the magical world, of War of the Ages 2. Louie, the family dog, who had been lying on her bed, sat up and cocked his head to one side, sensing her distraction. He barked excitedly, his tail wagging in anticipation.

"We'll see you at school, Milly," Ashley said from her side of the screen, moving Mirabel around in the pixelated ruins. "Make sure you tell us what your mum says about Athena's Shawl!"

"Of course," Milly replied, clicking her tongue at Louie to come over. He jumped off the bed and climbed into her lap, whimpering a little as he sought her attention. She scratched behind his ears and kissed the top of his head affectionately. "I'm not sure how much she knows, but it'll be interesting to hear her perspective, don't you think, Louie?" Louie gazed up at her, then licked her face in answer, his warm presence comforting her.

"Yeah, no doubt," Lucy's voice crackled through her slightly static-filled microphone. "But... do any of you feel weird playing this game now? Since we've met the characters in real life?"

"Well, it's still just a game," Ashley replied, her tone light-hearted. "War of the Ages 2 is still just a video game... I think."

"Milly!" her mum's voice rang out from downstairs, cutting through the moment. "Your breakfast is getting cold, darling!"

Milly quickly said goodbye to her friends and logged off from War of the Ages 2. She shut the computer off, making sure Louie didn't jump into Athena's Shawl while she was eating breakfast. Although... it would be a good excuse to miss school, she thought with a chuckle. Shaking the thought off, she went downstairs, Louie following eagerly, gnawing on one of his favourite chew toys.

"Good morning," Milly greeted, sitting down next to her younger sister, Fran, at the breakfast table. "How's your morning, Mum? Did you sleep well?"

Her mother, who had spent so long trapped in Athena's Shawl, looked surprisingly well-rested. Milly couldn't help but wonder how difficult it might be for her mother to adjust to normal life again, especially after being Deimos Asgard's prisoner.

"Oh, I slept fine, dear," her mother, Louise Martin, replied, placing a towering plate of flapjacks on the table, the sweet aroma wafting through the air. "It was wonderful to sleep in my own bed again."

Milly nodded, relieved to see her mother looking well despite everything. She glanced at Fran and Charlie, who were both staring at their mother with wide eyes, eager for an explanation. "So, why was Athena's Shawl in your bedroom, Mum?" Milly asked, unable to hold back any longer. "I'm still a bit confused about everything that happened."

"I've been wondering the same thing," Fran piped up, her curiosity evident.

Their father, John Martin, who had been pouring tea, set the cups down and placed a hand on Louise's shoulder. They shared a knowing look, a silent understanding passing between them.

"Go easy on your mum," he said, his voice warm and reassuring. "She's been through a lot."

He then sat down at the table, helping Charlie, the youngest, cut up his flapjacks with care.

Louise took a deep breath before speaking, her expression serious. "Athena's Shawl is an ancient and powerful artefact, passed down through generations. It has the power to protect its wearer and vanish when threatened. It only reappears in the presence of a worthy female descendant of Athena."

Milly nodded slowly, absorbing her mother's words. "Did you know you were a descendant of Athena?"

"No," Louise admitted, her voice tinged with uncertainty. "I didn't until recently. There's so much about my grandparents, and their parents, that I don't know."

Fran's eyes lit up with excitement. "So Athena's Shawl disappeared because Deimos Asgard got his hands on it?" She took a sip of tea, her mind racing with possibilities. "That's why it was with you, right?"

"Yes, Fran, that's pretty much it," Louise said, laughing a little as she smoothed the back of her youngest daughter's hair. "I found it in my wardrobe, but I had no idea of its power or how to use it. One evening, the light from my window hit the shawl, and before I knew it, I was absorbed into it."

Charlie leaned forward, his curiosity piqued. "And that's when Deimos Asgard found you?"

Louise nodded gravely, her expression turning serious. "Yes. He sensed the shawl's power, but he couldn't use it without my help. Of course, I refused to help him. He held me captive and tried to force me to reveal its secrets."

John Martin shuddered at the thought. "That man... I can't bear to think about it," he muttered, his voice filled with concern. Milly noticed the guilt in his eyes, probably regretting that he hadn't allowed the children to rescue their mother, , sooner, but at least they all understood now that it had been out of concern for their safety.

"Well, thankfully, you three showed incredible bravery," Louise said, smiling at her kids across the table, pride evident in her voice. "Along with Milly's friends, of course. And Louie, let's not forget him!"

"Oh, by the way, Milly," her mother added, a mischievous grin forming on her face. "That boy, Harry, couldn't take his eyes off you, could he?"

"Mum!" Milly exclaimed, her face flushing bright red at the unexpected comment. "What are you talking about? Harry and I are just friends." As she spoke, her cheeks reddened even more, and she felt a mix of embarrassment and amusement. Louie, sensing her discomfort, rubbed his back against her legs in a comforting gesture. Milly rewarded him with another chewie, grateful for his unwavering support.

Her mother laughed, clearly enjoying the moment. "Just teasing, sweetheart. Anyway, it's up to us to keep Athena's Shawl safe. We can't let it fall into the wrong hands again."

She polished off the last of her tea and flapjacks and stood up, her expression turning serious once more. "And yes, Milly, before you ask, you can keep Athena's Shawl in your bedroom. Just... be careful with it, alright?"

"I will, Mum," Milly said, grateful for her mother's trust. She glanced at the clock above the refrigerator and gasped, realising the time. "I'm going to be late for school!" She quickly washed her dish and dashed upstairs to change into her uniform, her heart racing as she hurried to get ready. Louie, who had been lying beneath the table, barked and bounded after her, eager to accompany her.

Once ready, Milly placed Louie in his favourite basket by the radiator and gave him one last treat before heading out the door to school, her mind still buzzing with thoughts of Athena's Shawl and the adventures that awaited her.

Milly met up with her best friends, Ashley and Lucy, outside John Wilkes Secondary School. Her hair was in its usual ponytail, though she had forgotten to wash her face in her rush. Lucy noticed immediately, her keen eyes catching every detail.

"You alright, Milly?" she asked, raising an eyebrow in concern. "You look a bit dishevelled."

"Rude," Ashley teased, laughing as she playfully punched Lucy lightly on the shoulder, a smile on her face.

"Oh, I'm fine," Milly giggled, brushing off their comments. "I just got caught up talking to my mum about you-know-what." She glanced around at the other students gathered on the front steps of the school, their laughter and chatter filling the air. They were deep in conversation, but Milly didn't want anyone overhearing her talk about Athena's Shawl. What her mum had said about making sure the shawl didn't fall into the wrong hands rang in her mind like a church bell, a constant reminder of the responsibility she now bore.

Perhaps that was why she was so quiet while walking to her first class of the day with Ashley and Lucy. At least it's history class, she thought, trying to focus on the positives. I don't have to think about anything else while I'm in history. After shuffling into the classroom, she made her way to her desk. Harry, sitting at the desk directly in front of hers, gave her a little smile when she walked in. When she smiled back at him, he blushed and quickly looked away to his friend, Chris, who was talking non-stop about War of the Ages 2, his enthusiasm infectious.

"Did you two end up playing War of the Ages 2 last night?" Ashley asked as she took her seat next to Milly, her voice filled with curiosity. "We were too tired after everything that happened... but Milly insisted we play this morning."

"We played for a bit," Chris replied, his tone casual. "Harry kept accidentally dying, though. We never got past the raid on Alexandria."

"In my defence," Harry said, rolling his eyes in mock annoyance. "I was distracted. Plus, it was my first time playing as Wolfstan. I'm not used to that character."

"Excuses, excuses," Chris grinned, clearly enjoying the banter.

Meanwhile, Milly's heart began to race. Harry played as Wolfstan? she thought, her mind racing with possibilities. But I always play as Wolfstan. Why is he so interested in playing as him all of a sudden? She began wondering if Harry's interest in Wolfstan might be because it was her favourite character. Maybe he thought playing as Wolfstan would give them something to talk about. Maybe he thought it would help him understand her better, too. She made a mental note to talk to Ashley and Lucy about it later, hoping she wasn't overthinking it.

Just then, the history teacher, Mr. Hayes, entered the classroom with his bag slung over his shoulder, his presence commanding attention. "Alright, settle down, class," he said, setting his bag on the floor and pulling out his lecture notes. "Today we're going to talk about Alexander the Great. I'm sure you've heard of him?" He smiled and wrote "Alexander the Great" on the whiteboard with a purple marker, the letters bold and clear. "He ruled over the ancient Greek kingdom of Macedon and was a feared conqueror." Milly quickly took out her notebook and pencil, eager for what she knew would be another fascinating lecture.

"Let's start with one of the most legendary battles in history, the war between Alexander the Great and King Porus in Punjab, India." Mr. Hayes described the rugged terrain, where the Hydaspes River wound through mountains and villages, painting a vivid picture with his words. "The Hydaspes, which is now known as the Jhelum River, played a major role in the battle. To reach King Porus, Alexander and his cavalry would have to cross the river, which was no easy task." He sifted through his notes and cleared his throat, preparing to delve deeper into the story.

"Both men were determined to win, knowing that the fate of their lands was at stake. But Alexander was a master strategist," Mr. Hayes continued, his voice full of admiration. "He knew a direct assault on Porus's army would be risky. So, he devised a daring plan to outsmart his opponent." The students leaned in, eager to learn about Alexander's tactics. "Night after night, Alexander scouted the river's edge until he discovered an uninhabited island upstream," Mr. Hayes went on, his enthusiasm infectious. "He gathered his soldiers and told them they would cross the river under cover of darkness, then launch a surprise attack on the Indian cavalry."

Milly's pencil was flying across the page as she took notes, her mind racing with excitement. She couldn't help but think of War of the Ages and the epic cutscene between Alexander the Great and King Porus after Alexander's victory. "Psst... it's just like in War of the Ages," Lucy whispered, leaning over to Milly's ear as if reading her mind, her voice barely above a whisper.

"The day of the battle dawned," Mr. Hayes said, giving Lucy a stern look, a hint of amusement in his eyes. "As the mist cleared, Alexander's forces descended upon Porus's camp." He described the clash of swords, the trumpeting of elephants, and the fierce determination of both Alexander and King Porus. "Despite King Porus's bravery," Mr. Hayes explained, "he couldn't defeat Alexander the Great. Alexander emerged victorious, but not without admiration for Porus, , who fought valiantly until the end." He took off his glasses and pulled out a handkerchief, wiping his face as he caught his breath.

The students leaned forward, hanging on his every word, captivated by the tale.

"Then what happened, Mr. Hayes?" Ashley asked, forgetting, as usual, to raise her hand, her curiosity getting the better of her.

Mr. Hayes smiled, clearly pleased with the engagement. "When Alexander returned to Babylon," he said, "he fell ill with a mysterious fever. He died in the arms of his loyal friend, Sisygambis, who he entrusted with burying him and safeguarding his riches." He put his glasses back on and shuffled through his notes again, preparing to conclude the lesson. "Rumour has it Alexander's tomb lies somewhere deep beneath the city of Alexandria, alongside his vast wealth. Many have tried to find it, but Sisygambis took great care to protect it from thieves. It's said she marked its location with ancient Persian symbols and used magic to guard it." Harry raised his hand, which seemed to please Mr. Hayes, , especially since Harry didn't usually pay much attention in class. "Yes, Harry?"

"Why did Alexander want Sisygambis to bury his riches with him?" Harry asked, his brow furrowed in thought. "And why didn't she just take them for herself after he died?" The class murmured in agreement, and Harry looked proud of himself for posing such a thought-provoking question. "I mean, he's dead, right? If Sisygambis or someone else stole the riches, how would he know?"

"Well..." Mr. Hayes said, crossing his arms and leaning against the desk. "The ancient Greeks were quite god-fearing. Alexander trusted Sisygambis to bury him in a tomb fit for a king, along with his treasures. Sisygambis was the mother of Darius III, and Alexander called her 'mother.' She likely never even considered taking the riches for herself. In fact, it's said she took her own life shortly after." The bell rang, signalling the end of class, and Mr. Hayes clasped his hands together, a smile breaking across his face. "Don't forget, you have a quiz on Friday. It should be easy as long as you've read Chapters 4 and 5, so I expect you all to do well!"

The rest of the school day went by without incident. Milly attended netball practice with Ashley and Lucy, changed back into her uniform, and began walking home alone, her mind still buzzing with thoughts of the day's lessons. She had barely taken a few steps away from the gymnasium when she ran into Harry, who had just finished football practice. He hadn't bothered to change out of his athletic gear; his hair was dripping with sweat, and his long football socks were caked in mud. Despite his state, he seemed genuinely happy to see Milly and, , to her slight surprise, , began walking with her.

"Hey, Milly," he said, his voice brightening her mood. "How was netball practice?"

Milly gave him a perplexed look. Harry had never shown much interest in things like that before. "It was alright, I guess," she replied, trying to gauge his interest. "We have a match coming up soon. How's football going?"

"Oh, you know," Harry said with his usual crooked grin, slicking back his hair with his hand. He tucked his hands behind his back, looking a bit awkward but endearing. "Can I ask you something?"

Milly's heart skipped a beat, her mind racing with possibilities. "Of course," she said, trying to hide the smile threatening to form on her face. She noticed the serious expression on Harry's face, however, and quickly shifted her tone. "What is it, Harry?"

Harry sighed, his expression turning somber. "It's my dad," he said, his voice dropping. "He... he got into some trouble."

"What kind of trouble?" Milly asked, unsure where this conversation was going. As they walked, she adjusted the straps of her book bag for comfort, kicking a stone along the pavement, her mind wandering as Harry gathered his thoughts. Milly had never been fond of Harry's dad due to how he treated Harry, but she knew Harry loved him deeply. He was always trying to impress his dad with his athletic skills, but no matter what he did, it never seemed enough. Her first instinct was to say, "If your dad's in trouble, he can shove it," but that felt too harsh, so she stayed quiet, patiently waiting for Harry to speak.

"Er..." he hesitated, his voice thick with emotion. "He owes this bloke some money. A lot of money."

"Oh," Milly said, stopping herself from kicking the stone. "How much money?"

"Several thousand pounds," Harry said, looking down, his expression troubled. He started explaining how his father had borrowed money from a loan shark a while ago, after losing a lot of money gambling and struggling to make mortgage payments. "It's not like he borrowed it all at once," Harry added, his voice tinged with frustration. "It just built up over time."

"What's he going to do?" Milly asked, her concern growing.

"Well, that's the problem," Harry said, his voice barely above a whisper. "He doesn't know what he's going to do. We don't know what to do. This bloke, the loan shark, is bad news, Milly. He's already come to the house twice demanding the money. I'm worried that, ..." Harry trailed off, clearing his throat as he fought back tears. He looked like he was holding back a flood of emotions. "I'm worried he's going to hurt my dad."

"Harry..." Milly placed her hand on his shoulder, trying to offer comfort.

"As much as my dad can be a prat sometimes," Harry continued, his voice trembling, "I don't want anything bad to happen to him. He's all I've got."

Milly was at a loss for words, her heart aching for him. "I... I'm sure it's going to be okay," she said, her voice steady. "But I'm confused. Wasn't there something you wanted to ask me?"

"Right," Harry said, shaking his head as if trying to clear his thoughts. "So... you know how you, your mum, and your sister can travel between worlds? Or time travel? I'm still not sure how Athena's Shawl works, but..." He trailed off, his eyes searching hers for understanding.

"Athena's Shawl is still a bit of a mystery to us," Milly said, her mind racing. "My mum, Fran, and I are all descendants of Athena, which is why the shawl ended up in our family. When we went into War of the Ages 2, it was hard to tell if we were physically inside the game or if we'd gone back in time. At the time, I thought we were definitely inside the game, since that's what Athena's Shawl projected when we jumped into it. But looking back, I'm not so sure."

"Maybe we should use Athena's Shawl again," Harry suggested, his eyes lighting up with excitement. "This time, to find Alexander's tomb and those riches Mr. Hayes mentioned."

Milly stared at him, disbelief written across her face. "Let me get this straight," she said, her voice incredulous. "You want to use Athena's Shawl to travel back in time, break into Alexander the Great's tomb, and steal his riches to help your dad pay back the loan shark?"

Harry grinned, his enthusiasm infectious. "Pretty much."

"Harry, come on," Milly said, shaking her head in disbelief. "Not only would that be an irresponsible way to use Athena's Shawl, but it just doesn't feel right,"

"This is exactly what I was talking about in class!" Harry threw his hands up, frustration evident in his tone. "Alexander the Great is dead. He doesn't need all that money!" As they turned the corner and Milly's house came into view, Harry grabbed her hand, making her heart race. "Look, you don't have to give me an answer now," he said, his voice earnest. "Just think about it, okay?" He let go of her hand and started walking back toward the school, turning around once more to add, "Also, it'd be cool to see Ancient Alexandria, don't you think?"

Milly stood there for a moment, her mind racing with thoughts of adventure, responsibility, and the weight of the choices before her.

2

WITH GREAT POWER

After dinner that night, Milly quietly ascended the stairs to her bedroom, her mind swirling with thoughts as she reflected on the serious conversation she had just had with Harry. Louie, her loyal companion, trailed behind her, whining softly as if he could sense the inner turmoil that was brewing within her. "Come on, boy," she said gently, lifting the ruddy-coloured dog into her arms and closing her bedroom door behind her with a soft click. She set Louie down on the bed, gave him a Louie Chewie as a treat, and lay down next to him, feeling the familiar comfort of his presence. With her fingers laced behind her head, she stared up at the ceiling, lost in thought. The sun was streaming through Athena's Shawl, casting a warm glow across the room, and Louie, who couldn't seem to settle down, kept looking at it longingly, as if he were eager for another adventure.

"Not now, Louie," Milly said, patting his head affectionately. "I need to think about what I'm going to do."

Louie huffed and nudged her hand with his nose, his big brown eyes filled with an earnestness that made her smile. Milly wondered why he wanted to venture back into the unknown so badly. She supposed he'd had a good time exploring the ancient temple and fighting giant spiders the last time they had used the shawl, but wasn't he tired? She smiled at him, silently promising Louie that she'd bring him along the next time she used Athena's Shawl. But she was still unsure about Harry's request. She knew stealing was wrong, even from a dead person. "In fact, there's a word for it," she muttered to herself. "Grave robbing." Despite her conflicted feelings, she couldn't shake her curiosity about Alexander's tomb. "And what about Harry? He's so worried about his dad..." She scratched Louie behind his ear, and he let out a heavy sigh, wagging his tail in appreciation. "I hated seeing him like that."

Not knowing what else to do, Milly got up from the bed and sat down at her computer, her fingers hovering over the keyboard. Maybe Ashley and Lucy will have some ideas, she thought. There's got to be another way for Harry's dad to pay back the loan shark. Come to think of it, that really shouldn't be Harry's responsibility! She shook her head as she turned on her computer and logged into Discord. The whole situation made her angry. Why did Harry feel like he owed his dad anything? Why did he have to be the one to save him? Then, she thought about her mum and how she'd been desperate to save her from the evil clutches of Deimos Asgard. She was closer to her mother than Harry was with his dad, sure, but that didn't matter. "I guess when it comes to my family," Milly said aloud, "I would do anything to protect them. Maybe Harry's the same way." Louie sat up on the bed and barked, as if agreeing with her.

Turning her attention back to Discord, she noticed Ashley was online and immediately started typing a message. "Get on voice chat," she wrote. "I have something to tell you." Milly put on her headphones, and almost immediately, Ashley invited her into a call.

"Hey, Milly," Ashley greeted her cheerfully. "Hold on, let me get Lucy in here. She's probably busy playing Hitman 3."

"No doubt," Milly said, chuckling at the thought of Lucy's new obsession with the game. "Were you about to play War of the Ages 2?"

"I was thinking about it," Ashley replied. "But I have no idea how we're going to get into the caliph's secret treasure room. It's funny to think about

Catalina, Wolfstan, Mirabel, and Faramund just standing around, waiting for something to happen."

"Yeah..." Milly said, her mind racing as she considered the implications of their last adventure. "About that..."

Just then, Lucy joined the call, her voice cutting through the static. "This better be good, Milly," she said, not bothering with any hellos. "I was in the middle of a really good run in Hitman 3."

"Sorry," Milly said, her tone serious. "But this is important. It's about Harry."

"When is it not about Harry?" Lucy asked, her tone teasing. Milly was fairly sure she was joking, but it was hard to tell through the static in her microphone. "Alright then. Out with it."

Milly took a deep breath, feeling the weight of her words. "So, I ran into Harry after netball practice today, and he told me something really serious. He said his dad owes a lot of money to a loan shark, and if he doesn't pay it back soon, the bloke might do something really bad, ..."

"Wait, slow down, Milly," Ashley said, her voice filled with concern. "How did Harry's dad get involved with a loan shark?"

"What's a loan shark?" Lucy asked, her curiosity evident.

"You're the one who watches all those true crime shows, Lucy," Ashley said, exasperated. "You don't know what a loan shark is?"

"No... that's why I'm asking," Lucy replied, her tone defensive.

Milly could practically hear Ashley rolling her eyes through her headset. "A loan shark is someone who lends money but charges insanely high interest rates. If the person who borrowed money can't pay it back, well... things can get violent. Not always, but sometimes. Either way, I'm pretty sure it's illegal."

"It is," Milly confirmed. "Harry said it's a really sketchy situation, but his dad lost a bunch of money gambling and had to borrow from this bloke to keep up with payments on his house and stuff."

"Gosh," Ashley said, her voice filled with sympathy. "Poor Harry. That's heavy."

"Yep," Milly agreed, her heart aching for her friend. "And guess what? He wants to use Athena's Shawl to go back in time and raid Alexander the Great's tomb... as if he's bloody Lara Croft or something. He said, and I quote, 'Alexander the Great is dead. He doesn't need all that money!'"

"Well... he's not wrong," Lucy said, her tone thoughtful. "Alexander the Great is dead."

"Is that why he was acting so strange in history class today?" Ashley asked, her brow furrowing in concern. "He must not be thinking straight."

Milly nodded in agreement, though her friends couldn't see her. "I know," she said. "You should have seen the look on his face when he told me. He thinks it's the only way to get his family out of debt, but... I don't know. It doesn't feel right."

"He's desperate," Lucy said, her voice softening. "Understandably. I mean, he doesn't exactly have time to get a job and help his dad pay the loan shark back, does he? That would take forever. Has this bloke shown up at Harry's house?"

"Harry said he's been there twice already, threatening his dad," Milly told her, swallowing a lump in her throat, her eyes starting to well up with tears. "What if he hurts Harry? I care about him. I know you guys think it's just a stupid crush, but..." she trailed off, her voice barely above a whisper.

There was a brief silence before Ashley spoke softly. "Milly, it's okay to care. Harry needs someone to look out for him, especially with everything his family's going through," she said gently. "And we care about him too, you know? He's our friend."

Milly smiled, feeling a sense of camaraderie. "So, what do you guys think I should do? Should I use Athena's Shawl to help Harry?"

"Only if you plan on taking us with you," Lucy said, her tone playful yet serious.

"I reckon my brother and sister will want to come too," Milly said, propping her elbows up on her desk and holding her head in her hands. From the bed, Louie barked loudly, as if he were ready for the adventure. "And Louie, of course," she added, a smile creeping onto her face.

Ashley sighed, her voice filled with determination. "I'm in," she said. "But let's prepare a bit more before jumping into the shawl this time, okay?"

After saying goodbye to her friends and logging off Discord, Milly went downstairs to make a cup of tea, her mind still racing with thoughts of their plan. Louie checked the bedrooms to see who was around before following her, his excitement about going back into the strange world of War of the Ages 2 evident in his wagging tail. Milly's parents and siblings were sitting on the couch watching a movie, giving Milly a bit more time to think. Although her mum supported her using Athena's Shawl, the idea of telling her , , why made Milly anxious. Hey, Mum, Harry asked me if I wanted to go grave robbing with him. Oh, and you're wondering whose grave? Alexander the Great's, she thought to herself, shaking her head at the absurdity of it all. Milly put the kettle on. "Does anyone want tea?" she called out.

"I'll have some, darling!" her mother replied, her voice cheerful. "Can you bring over that box of Jammie Dodgers too?"

"Okay, Mum!" While brewing the tea, Milly grabbed the half-empty box of Jammie Dodgers from the kitchen cabinet and popped one into her mouth, savouring the sweet taste. Maybe I shouldn't tell my parents the real reason I want to use Athena's Shawl, she thought, her mind racing with possibilities. She poked her head into the living room and glanced at the television screen. They were watching Spider-Man, and had just gotten to the scene where Uncle Ben passes away in Peter Parker's arms.

"With great power comes great responsibility," Uncle Ben said, his words resonating deeply with Milly. It was a scene she practically had memorised by now, since Spider-Man was Charlie's favourite movie. You've got to be kidding me, she thought, feeling the weight of the moment.

She prepared her mum's tea, two sugars and a splash of milk, just the way she liked it, and tried to come up with a convincing story for her parents. She wasn't particularly good at lying, so she'd need to stay calm and casual. Maybe I can say I'm doing a history project on Alexander the Great, she thought, her heart racing as she tucked the box of Jammie Dodgers under her arm and walked into the living room, carrying the tea. Keep it together, she reminded herself, as the teacup trembled slightly in her hand. Oh, Harry... why did you have to drag me into this mess?

"Here's your tea, Mum," she said, placing the cup into her mother's hands. "And your favourite biscuits." Louie, too, seemed intrigued by the biscuits. He laid his head on Louise Martin's lap and whimpered, his big eyes pleading for a treat.

"Thank you, sweetheart," her mum replied, gently nudging Louie aside and pulling a Jammie Dodger from the box. Milly sat down beside her siblings, who were both completely absorbed in Spider-Man, even though they watched it almost every week. She leaned in closer to them and whispered, "Hey, I've got an idea for a fun adventure."

Fran's eyes lit up with excitement. "What is it?" she asked eagerly.

Milly glanced at her mum, who was happily dipping a biscuit into her tea. "Hey, Mum?" she said, her heart pounding in her chest. "My history teacher said we have to do a report on a historical figure."

"Oh?" Her mother turned to her, her interest piqued. "That sounds right up your alley, Milly. Who are you doing your report on?"

"Alexander the Great," Milly replied, trying to sound steady and confident. "I was thinking... maybe I could use Athena's Shawl to go into my video game and learn a bit more about him. The War of the Ages 2 characters are in Ancient Alexandria right now, which is where Alexander the Great was supposedly buried."

Charlie's eyes widened in amazement. "That sounds amazing!" he exclaimed, his enthusiasm infectious. "Can we come with you?"

Fran nodded eagerly, her excitement bubbling over. "Please, Milly! It would be so much fun!"

Louie barked happily, then started chasing his tail and rolling around on the carpet at Milly's feet, adding to the lively atmosphere.

Milly hesitated, once again torn between wanting to keep her siblings and Louie safe and including them in the adventure. "I don't know, guys. It might be dangerous."

"We won't get in the way, I promise," Fran pleaded, her eyes wide with hope.

"We'll be your backup team, just in case anything goes wrong," Charlie added, his voice filled with determination.

Louie nudged Milly's knee with his nose and huffed dramatically, as if saying, Come on, Milly. Take a chance.

"Now, hold on just a minute," their father called from across the room, his tone serious. "Milly, I'm glad you're keen on history, but do you really need to use Athena's Shawl for a report on Alexander the Great? Don't you think you're going a bit overboard?" He glanced at Louise, who was shooting daggers at him with her eyes. "What?" he said, throwing his hands up in exasperation. "I'm sure Milly will do just fine without it! Are you really going to let her endanger herself and the little ones every time she has a history project?"

"We're not going to be in danger, Dad," Milly said, feeling a pang of hurt at his words. "And I would never put Fran and Charlie in any danger."

"You need to have more faith in our kids, John," Louise said firmly. "You said that yourself just the other night. I know you're just worried, but you shouldn't assume Milly will put Fran and Charlie in harm's way."

"I'm sorry," John stammered, his expression softening. "I, I didn't mean it like that,"

"You weren't there when they rescued me," Louise continued, her voice unwavering. "I've seen what Milly, Fran, and Charlie can do. They've proved themselves, just like Louie. I don't doubt for a second that they'll be fine this time around too." John fell silent, his expression thoughtful. He sank back into the couch, trying to focus on the movie. Louise turned to Milly, giving her a serious look. "I trust you, Milly," she said, her voice steady. "But I need you to promise me you won't do anything reckless." She gestured at Peter Parker's face on the screen. "'With great power comes great responsibility,' right?"

Milly nodded, her guilt gnawing at her, but there was no turning back now. She was determined to help Harry, no matter what it took. "I'll be careful, Mum," she said, her voice firm. "I'll... I'll make good choices. I promise."

"I know you will, darling," her mother said, her expression softening. "When are you all going?"

"Um... I was thinking tomorrow," Milly replied, her heart racing with anticipation. "Or maybe the day after. Ashley, Lucy, and Harry are coming too. We want to be properly prepared this time."

"Well then," her mum said, beaming with pride, "I'll pack you some brown-bag lunches. Wouldn't want you going hungry. That includes you too, Louie."

The next day, after school, Milly met with Ashley, Lucy, and Harry to finalise their plan. They found a quiet spot in the courtyard where they wouldn't be overheard, the sun shining brightly above them. Harry was overjoyed that Milly had decided to help him, and Ashley and Lucy seemed eager for another adventure, their excitement palpable.

"Will you all be ready by this evening?" Milly asked them, her heart pounding with anticipation.

Harry smiled, his enthusiasm infectious. "I'm ready now," he said, his eyes sparkling with excitement. "At the risk of sounding like a nerd, I'm actually excited to see Ancient Alexandria."

"We need to stick together and watch each other's backs," Lucy said, her tone serious yet encouraging.

Ashley wrung her hands, looking a little nervous. "Right, that's the most important thing," she said. "And remember, we're doing this to help Harry with his dad's loan shark problem," she shot Harry a knowing glance. "It might get a bit chaotic, God knows it did last time, but let's try to stay focused on the mission."

Milly nodded, her determination solidifying. "Let's meet at my house after dinner. Fran and Charlie are in, and Louie's ready for an adventure too. Don't forget to wear clothes that'll help you blend in."

The final bell rang, and the four of them went their separate ways, agreeing to meet later that evening, each of them filled with a sense of purpose and excitement.

Milly walked home, her heart filled with determination. The sun was a brilliant orange in the sky, like a freshly cracked egg yolk, casting a warm glow over everything. It was the perfect day to use Athena's Shawl. Louie greeted her at the door, along with Fran, Charlie, and their mum. As promised, Mum had packed brown-bag lunches for them, ham sandwiches, apple slices, and crisps, which Milly, Fran, and Charlie tucked into their backpacks with care.

"I've made lunch for Louie and your friends, too, Milly," her mother said, handing her an armful of brown paper bags. "I packed a nice bone and several Louie chewies for Louie and an extra sandwich for Harry. He's a growing boy."

"I'm a growing boy too, Mum," Charlie piped up, his voice filled with enthusiasm.

"Yes, you are," Louise replied, crouching down to Charlie's level. "But your eyes are usually bigger than your stomach, sweetheart." She tousled his hair affectionately and clasped her hands together. Despite her confidence in her children, she couldn't hide a small hint of worry.

Milly noticed this. "Are you okay, Mum?" she asked, her concern evident.

"Oh, I'm fine," Louise said, waving off Milly's concern with a smile. "It's just... there's something I want to talk to you about. Something I haven't told your father." She was met with puzzled looks from all three of her children. "Maybe it's easier if I show you," she said, her tone serious. "Follow me." Louie trotted after them, his tail wagging in excitement. They followed their mother outside into the garden, which was, admittedly, looking a bit neglected. Milly's dad didn't have much of a green thumb, so the roses, daisies, and peonies had wilted in Louise's absence.

"Okay, now... don't be alarmed," she said, kneeling beside a withered rose bush. She closed her eyes and held her hand over one of the dead roses, her brow furrowing in concentration. To Milly's surprise, the rose bloomed back to life, its pink petals regaining their colour, and the once-dry leaves, , turned a healthy green, vibrant and full of life.

"Wow!" Fran gasped, her eyes wide with wonder. "Mum... since when can you bring plants back to life?"

Milly was too stunned to speak, and Charlie was equally speechless, while Louie sniffed the revived rose suspiciously, his head tilting in confusion.

"I didn't know I had this power until recently," Louise explained, her voice steady yet filled with awe. "Your dad accidentally killed a spider the other night, and when I went to dispose of it, I was shocked to find it came back to life in my palm! At first, I thought maybe your dad didn't actually kill it, but then I started noticing other things." She revived the other roses on the bush, one by one, , as they bloomed into vibrant pink and white flowers, filling the air with their sweet fragrance.

Milly regained her composure, her curiosity piqued. "Like what, Mum?" she asked, eager to understand more.

"Well, like this," Louise gestured to the rose bush, her eyes sparkling with excitement. "You know how much I love my flowers. After the spider incident, I thought... maybe I have healing powers. I am a descendant of a goddess, after all." She paused, her expression turning serious. "I can't heal the entire garden at once, though," she added, her shoulders slumping slightly. "This power... it makes me tired."

"Why are you telling us this?" Charlie asked, his brow furrowed in confusion. "And why haven't you told Dad?"

"Your dad won't understand," Louise replied, her voice firm yet gentle. "Or maybe I'm just not ready to tell him. But I'm telling you because you're also descendants of Athena. You might have powers of your own that you haven't discovered yet."

Milly nodded, her mind racing with possibilities. Her dad had always been overly logical, and the idea of special powers would probably be too much for him to handle. "So, what now?" Milly asked, her curiosity bubbling over. "If I have a power... how will I know?"

Louise stood up, brushing the dirt from her hands. "You'll just know," she said, her tone encouraging. "But... maybe you're not old enough to discover it yet. Or maybe you're meant to dig deep and find it within yourself."

"Do you think we'll have healing powers, like you?" Fran asked, her eyes shining with hope.

"I don't know, darling," her mother replied, her expression thoughtful. "I'm not sure if any of you will have powers. We'll just have to wait and see." She smoothed Fran's hair and smiled at all three of them. "While you're in Ancient Alexandria, as mad as that sounds, pay attention to how you feel. If anything unusual happens, make sure you're responsible."

"We will, Mum," Charlie said, his voice filled with determination.

"You probably don't even have powers, Charlie," Fran teased, her tone playful.

"I guess not, "

"Then why would you have powers?" Fran pressed, her eyes sparkling with mischief.

"Fran, be nice," Louise said, her tone firm yet affectionate. "Charlie could very well have powers. He's the first male child in my family since forever. We don't fully understand how Athena's Shawl works, and it could be that anyone who's been in the Shawl develops powers eventually. Remember, Deimos Asgard had powers." She kissed Charlie's head and bent down to pick up Louie, who was wagging his tail excitedly. "Who knows? Maybe Louie has powers, too. Only time will tell." She kissed Louie and set him down. "Make sure to bring his leash," she added as she started back towards the house. "I don't want him getting lost in Ancient Alexandria."

Milly felt a surge of excitement at the thought of their upcoming adventure, her mind racing with possibilities. The idea of discovering her own powers, alongside her friends and family, filled her with a sense of purpose. As they headed back inside, she couldn't help but wonder what awaited them in Ancient Alexandria and how their journey would unfold. With a determined heart, she resolved to face whatever challenges lay ahead, ready to embrace the unknown and protect those she cared about.

3

INTO THE UNKNOWN

The group, Fran, Charlie, Ashley, Lucy, Harry, and Louie, were squeezed together in Milly's bedroom, eagerly waiting for her to start *War of the Ages 2*. Charlie perched on the edge of Milly's bed, swinging his legs in excitement, while Fran sat with arms crossed, sighing dramatically and rolling her eyes, clearly impatient.

"What's taking so long, Milly?" she grumbled. "I'm getting bored."

"Just a bit longer," Milly replied. "This game has a bit of a loading time... and... ah, there we go!" The screen flickered before it fully formed Ancient Alexandria, with Captain Catalina, Wolfstan, Mirabel, and Faramund exactly where they had left them last time.

"Do you have the corner of Athena's Shawl that you ripped off, Fran? And that picture of Mum and

Dad?" Milly asked. "We need to make sure we can get back safely."

"Yep," Fran confirmed, patting her book bag.

"Good," Milly said, taking Fran's hand. The sunlight streamed through the mystical white cloth hanging in front of her window, and once again, the shadows of the four crusader knights danced across it. "Alright, everyone hold hands," she instructed, gathering Louie into her arms. "Charlie, grab my elbow."

After a bit of awkward shuffling, they formed a chain across the room, all fingers intertwined.

"Okay, on three. One... two... three!"

With a touch to the cloth, Milly felt herself falling. Her siblings clung to her desperately, and the others screamed as they tumbled alongside her. Milly squeezed her eyes shut, hoping that the ground wouldn't be too harsh. Just before they hit, they seemed to hover momentarily in the air. Milly wondered if she'd imagined it, perhaps Fran or , Charlie had done something, but a second later, they landed with a heavy thud on a dirt path. Fran landed right on top of her, and Louie, thrilled to be back on solid ground, barked and started licking their faces.

One by one, they got up and brushed themselves off. Athena's Shawl had transported them to a completely new place, as expected. The hustle and bustle of Ancient Alexandria surrounded them, , vendors haggling over prices, the rumbling sounds of distant chariots, and the intoxicating scent of exotic spices. Milly could hardly believe her eyes. She tightened her grip on Louie's leash, as she could tell he was eager to bolt.

"Easy, boy," she muttered. "There are lots of people here. I promised Mum I wouldn't lose you again."

Ashley gasped. "I can't believe it. We're actually here!"

"It doesn't look very war-torn," Lucy commented, squinting at a group of children playing a pretend game a few metres away. "In *War of the Ages 2*, weren't the crusaders storming the city? I wonder where Catalina and the others are."

"Maybe Athena's Shawl brought us past that part of time," Milly mused, noticing signs of destruction, broken clay and splintered wood, scattered around nearby buildings. "Er... at least a little bit. Let's have a look around."

Cautiously, the group started heading toward the heart of the city, where, according to their textbooks, the caliph's extravagant palace was supposed to stand out like a sore thumb, . The closer they got to the city's centre, the more they saw signs of recent damage from the crusade that had taken place there just weeks, , or, possibly days, before. Buildings had visible scars, and the air was thick with an underlying tension.

"Wow," Harry breathed. "This is amazing."

"It really is," Milly agreed. "Do you think the entrance to Alexander's tomb is nearby?"

"It's probably near the palace, right?" Ashley asked. "Didn't Mr. Hayes say that?"

Fran, who had been quietly taking in the ancient surroundings, spoke up. "I bet there are secret passages and hidden chambers in Alexander's tomb just waiting to be discovered!"

"You're probably right," Milly said. "That's why we need to find Catalina and the others. They'll be able to help us. I've done some research on ancient Persian symbols, and I brought a list along."

With renewed determination, the group set off in search of their companions. They passed through bustling marketplaces, admired a gorgeous temple with statues and intricate carvings, and navigated narrow alleyways that seemed to whisper with secrets. Louie tugged on the leash toward a street vendor selling what appeared to be juicy slices of meat, eager to get a taste.

"Hold on, Louie," Milly said. "We've got your favourite 'Louie Chewies' for later."

As they weaved through the labyrinthine streets, Milly couldn't help but marvel at the city's history. Everywhere they turned, she could almost hear the stories of past conquests, the legends of ancient gods, and the whispers of treasures long hidden. She had been uncertain about their mission before, but now, standing in the heart of Ancient Alexandria, her doubts seemed to vanish.

Finally, after what felt like an adventure in itself, Milly spotted a familiar figure in the distance. Captain Catalina stood tall, confident, and ready for action, her throwing knives gleaming in the sunlight. Mirabel, Wolfstan, and Faramund were by her side, offering their presence as reassurance.

"There they are!" Milly called out. "Captain Catalina!" She waved to get her attention.

Catalina turned, a wide grin spreading across her face as she recognised Milly and the group. "Milly! It's good to see you." She jogged over to them, with Mirabel, Wolfstan, and Faramund following close behind. "What brings you to the great city of Alexandria?"

Milly's heart raced as Mirabel enveloped her in a tight hug. "We're here to find Alexander the Great's tomb," Milly explained. "Harry, , " she gestured to

Harry, ", his dad is having some serious financial troubles, so we thought... well, Alexander's been gone for ages, right? He doesn't need all that treasure." She paused, looking around. "There's treasure in Alexander's tomb, right? That's not just a legend?"

"We were originally searching for the caliph's treasure," Wolfstan chimed in, "but maybe Alexander's tomb is here. If it is, his treasure would be enormous. The question is... where is it, and how do we get inside?"

"We were hoping you could help us find that out," Lucy added.

"Yeah... about that," Catalina began. "We've been trying to break into the caliph's treasure room for weeks. Nothing's worked. We may have to return to King Jason empty-handed... and I suspect he'll be very annoyed,"

"You've been trying to break into a treasure room for weeks?" Harry interrupted, wide-eyed. "Will you help us find Alexander's tomb and treasure room? It can't be that hard to bypass the traps and tricks set by Alexander's friend, right?" Catalina gave him a blank stare. "We... learned about it in history class," he muttered.

"The tomb of Alexander is protected by the gods," Mirabel said solemnly. "Athena and Apollo, I believe. If the gods don't want you somewhere..." She shrugged. "Sorry, Milly. Unless you find a clue and have some magical way to bypass the gods' protections, we're not sure how we can help."

Milly looked at Fran and Charlie. Could one of them thwart the gods and bypass their defences? She doubted it. But as her mother had said, there was no way of knowing if they had powers, or what those powers might be. She glanced at Ashley and Lucy, wishing she had already told them about her own potential special abilities. But she wasn't sure how to broach the subject, especially with Lucy, who would likely tease her. She decided to hold off, at least for now.

"We'll find it," Milly said, her voice filled with confidence. "And we'll find a way inside. I know we will."

"How can you be sure?" Faramund asked, tapping his foot impatiently against the dirt. "What do you kids have planned?"

"Well, we can't just give up," Harry replied, stepping forward. "We haven't even tried yet! I know you've been trying to get into the caliph's room for weeks, but we've got to see if there's anything we can do to get into Alexander's tomb. If I don't get that money to help my dad pay off that bloke... I..." He trailed off, wiping angry tears from his eyes. Milly hadn't even realised he'd been crying. "There has to be a way. We've got the clues Mr. Hayes gave us. We've come all this way. I'm not leaving until we've tried everything." He started walking along the dirt path as if he knew exactly where he was going. "Come on," he urged. "Standing around isn't going to help."

"You're going the wrong way," Catalina said, hands on her hips. "That's not going to do any good, either. Follow me, children." She beckoned them forward. "The entrance to the caliph's tomb is behind the palace."

It didn't take long for Milly to realise that Captain Catalina was leading them away from Alexander's palace, rather than towards it. As they turned a corner and entered what appeared to be a small neighbourhood, or rather, a collection of haphazardly constructed mud-brick houses, Milly tapped Catalina on the shoulder. "Um... where are we going? I thought the palace was at the centre of the city."

Catalina turned to her with a reassuring smile. "Trust me, Milly. There's a reason for this detour."

Milly was sceptical, but her curiosity got the better of her. She and the others followed Catalina, Mirabel, Faramund, and Wolfstan as they approached a tiny, witchy-looking hut at the end of the dirt road. Catalina knocked, and after a moment, a large wooden door creaked open, revealing an elderly woman with long, white hair, tattered clothing, and bags under her kind brown eyes.

"Catalina, deary!" she exclaimed, throwing her arms around Catalina, who was at least a foot taller than the old woman. "It's been too long!"

"We've only been gone a few hours," Catalina said, hugging her back.

"Come in, come in, all of you," the old woman beckoned, gesturing for them to follow her inside. Fran made a face upon seeing the woman's yellowed fingernails and hid behind Milly. "You've come just in time," the woman said as they entered. "I'm making Loukoumades."

Milly had no idea what "loukoumades" were, but the smell wafting from the woman's ancient cooking pot seemed somewhat familiar. Doughnuts, she thought, exchanging knowing glances with Fran and Charlie. Their mother always treated them to doughnuts on Saturdays, then they would walk around the park near their house and feed the ducks bits of bread. Or, at least... their mother used to do this before she was kidnapped by Deimos Asgard. Milly wondered if things would ever really be the same now that her mother was back. She hoped so.

While Catalina and the old woman exchanged pleasantries, Milly took the opportunity to look around the small house. The walls were lined with faded tapestries that seemed to tell stories of people from the past: Alexander the Great, Darius III, King Porus. Tattered paintings of gods and goddesses adorned the walls as well, Artemis, Apollo, Athena. Milly was beginning to understand why Catalina had brought them here. Perhaps this old woman, despite, her eccentricities, could help them figure out how to access Alexander's tomb.

Meanwhile, Louie was circling the loukoumades. The old woman was frying them in hot oil, which made Milly worry for Louie's safety. "Louie!" she said, tugging at his lead. He reluctantly sat down next to her feet. "Good boy," she said, shrugging off her bookbag to fetch the bone her mum had packed for Louie. "Want your bone?" Faramund and Wolfstan were watching Milly and Louie with unmistakable smirks on their faces.

"What are you two looking at?" Milly asked them as she handed Louie his bone. The little dog happily took it between his teeth and lay down to chew.

"Oh, nothing," Wolfstan said with a grin. "Your dog just makes me laugh... he's so spoiled."

"He sure is!" Milly agreed. "My mum's to blame for that."

Just then, Catalina cleared her throat, and everyone turned to look at her. "Okay, so... Wolfstan, Faramund, and Mirabel have already met her, obviously," Catalina said, gesturing to the old woman and placing a hand on her shoulder. "But this is Agnes. Back in her day, she was quite a talented archaeologist. We met her about a week ago, after... well, storming the city." Agnes gave Catalina a disapproving look. "But that's in the past now," Catalina added with a grin. "We didn't exactly have a place to stay, so she took us in. In exchange for her hospitality, we've been helping her with chores and whatnot."

"We've also been looking for her cat," Mirabel added, sounding slightly annoyed but still smiling. "Agnes said she ran off quite some time ago." She leaned in and whispered something in Ashley's ear.

Ashley smiled sweetly and tucked her hands into her pockets. "Is that what Louie's sniffing around for? He has a very keen sense of smell. We'll find her, Miss Agnes," she said, addressing the old woman. "Don't worry, I think Louie has the scent."

Agnes stood by her cooking pot, wringing her hands. She crouched down to check on the loukoumades. "It's been a while since I've had so many people in my home," she said. "Actually, I don't think I've ever had this many people in my home at once." She picked up a gnarled wooden spoon and began scooping the golden-brown loukoumades onto a ceramic plate. "You'll really help me find my Iris?"

She looked up at Ashley. "Catalina and her friends haven't had any luck, but I just know she's somewhere in the city... I've been praying to the gods that she wasn't hurt during the crusade."

"I'm sure she's fine," Mirabel reassured her. "Cats can be tricky to find, but she'll turn up eventually." She exchanged a look with Faramund, who gave her a tiny shrug that no one else seemed to notice.

Agnes nodded and hoisted herself up from the floor, precariously balancing the plate of loukoumades on her forearm. "You must all help me eat these loukoumades, dearies," she said to Catalina, who took the plate and began to pass it around the room. "I always make far too many." Louie, who had been happily chewing on his bone, suddenly looked up and barked loudly.

"Oh!" Agnes jumped at least five feet in the air. "That's a strange-looking dog. I didn't even notice he was here."

"You think he's strange-looking?" Milly shook her head at Louie and pointed at his bone. "No loukoumades for you, Louie. I don't think they're good for dogs." Louie huffed, clearly disagreeing with that sentiment. "You have a perfectly good bone right there!" Milly said. "Why do I always find myself arguing with you, Louie Roi?" Ashley and Lucy began laughing, and Fran and Charlie, unable to contain themselves, collapsed into a fit of giggles on the floor.

"I've never seen a dog like that," Agnes said, squinting at Louie. "Actually... you all look quite strange." She eyed their odd-looking clothes. "Where are you from? Which side of the war are you on?" Her voice had suddenly turned defensive. She grabbed her gnarled walking stick and pointed it at them like a staff. "I'm not afraid to use this thing!" she threatened. "The gods are on my side, you know! I pray to them every day!"

"Easy, Agnes," Catalina said, stepping between Milly and the old woman. "You know me by now. I wouldn't bring anyone untrustworthy into your home."

Agnes lowered her walking stick and scratched her head with her yellowed fingernails, looking slightly confused. "Right..." she mumbled. "Sorry, dear. I'm just an old woman, and I'm not used to so many strangers."

"Just an old woman, eh?" Catalina raised an eyebrow and smiled, placing her hands on her hips. "I think we both know you're not just an old woman, Agnes."

Agnes's demeanour shifted. She looked at Catalina with a mixture of surprise and amusement. "How did you know?" she asked, her voice laced with mischief.

"Just a hunch," Catalina said with a grin.

The old woman laughed. "Ah, well... best not leave you and your companions in the dark any longer."

Milly and her friends exchanged curious glances. Harry, who'd been quiet up until now, leaned in, his eyes wide with intrigue. "What do you mean?"

Agnes grinned broadly and gestured to a nearby table where an ancient-looking tome lay open. "I have a few tricks up my sleeve, you see. I may not look like it, but I have a gift for magic."

"You look exactly like you can do magic," Faramund remarked, eyeing her with a knowing smile.

"I knew it!" Fran said, rushing over to get a closer look at the ancient tome. "You're a witch! That's why you live in a secluded hut and have long, yellow fingernails!"

"Fran!" Milly said, slightly aghast. "You can't just say things like that!"

"Why not?" Fran shrugged.

"Because it's rude!"

To Milly's surprise, Agnes laughed and gave Fran a gentle pat on the head. "Where I live and what I look like has nothing to do with my ability to use magic," she said. "I suppose you've read about witches that look like me in storybooks? You should see my sister, Agatha. All the men think she's a sight for sore eyes. Of course, Agatha never comes to visit anymore. She lives in the west, near the ocean. The silly girl got herself a job guarding the entrance to the underworld with the gorgons..." She shook her head. "I prefer to use my magic for scientific and archaeological purposes. I use it to uncover what happened in history." She blew dust off the large tome in front of her, making Fran cough. "Did you bring your oddly-dressed friends here for a reason, Catalina? Or are you just here to enjoy my loukoumades?"

"Uh... both, I suppose," Catalina said. "Milly is a magic-wielder as well. I know this might be hard for you to believe, but these kids and their dog are actually from the future. That's why they look so out of place."

"Oh!" Agnes's eyes sparkled. She suddenly rushed up to Milly and began pinching her cheeks. "Fascinating! I must document this for my research. Would you mind if I asked you a few questions?"

"Slow down, Agnes," Catalina interrupted. "I'm sure Milly would be happy to answer your questions, but we have some questions of our own, questions that I'm fairly sure only you can answer." She looked at Milly, nudging her chin towards her bookbag. "Why don't you show her the information you found about those Persian symbols, Milly?"

"Okay," Milly said, rifling through her bag until she found the crumpled list of symbols. She'd done her best to copy them from her history textbook, though she wasn't the best artist. She hoped her renditions of the Persian symbols would be clear enough for Agnes to identify.

Agnes's expression shifted as she studied the list of Persian symbols that Milly had brought with her. She ran her finger over the ancient characters, her eyes narrowing as she concentrated. "These symbols are indeed significant," she murmured. "They're the key to unlocking the secrets of Alexander's tomb. But deciphering them will require more than just knowledge of the Persian language."

Milly's heart began to race with anticipation. "Can you understand them? Can you help us figure out how to access Alexander's tomb?" she asked eagerly.

Agnes nodded slowly. "I can certainly try... though I'm not entirely fond of strangers from the future attempting to raid the tomb of our great leader," she added, shaking her head. "Be warned, though. Unravelling the mysteries of these symbols won't be easy. They're imbued with ancient magic, and it's going to take some time for me to decipher them."

"That's okay," Milly said, her voice steady. "Take all the time you need."

"Well... maybe you could hurry it up a bit," Harry interjected. "You see, the reason we want to break into Alexander's tomb is,"

"Because we're doing a history project," Milly quickly cut in, shooting him a warning look. There was no way this old woman would approve of them raiding her great leader's tomb for his riches. "For school. I really want to make an 'A'."

Harry gave her a quizzical look but remained silent. Milly relaxed her expression and offered him a subtle smile, as if to say: *I'll explain everything later.*

"I have no idea what you mean by 'make an 'A'," Agnes remarked, raising an eyebrow. "But as long as your intentions are purely educational and you show respect for the caliph, I have no objection. You'll, of course, have to be quite sneaky about this. After the crusaders left, , well, except for these four, ," she gestured to Catalina, Mirabel, Wolfstan, and Faramund, "the Alexandrians began to rebuild their city. By now, there are more guards protecting the palace and the entrance to the caliph's tomb than ever before. You'll probably need to get some new clothes, too..." She smirked at Milly's attire. "People will be suspicious, but fresh clothing might help you blend in."

"Oh... right," Milly said, feeling slightly stung by Agnes's words, but knowing deep down that the woman was right. She glanced at her friends, noting the mix of excitement and apprehension on their faces.

"Very well," Mirabel said, stepping forward. "I'll help you find some new clothes. In the meantime, perhaps Agnes can work on deciphering the Persian symbols. What do you think, Agnes?"

"I'll do my best," the old woman said. "Keep an eye out for Iris, though. She's grey and white, with blue eyes."

"So you've told us," Mirabel said, offering her a kind smile. "We'll let you know if we see her." She motioned for Milly and the others to follow her, and they left the little house, , along with the lingering smell of loukoumades, , and stepped back out into the streets.

Mirabel led them through the winding lanes of the neighbourhood until they arrived at a row of modest mud-brick houses. She stopped in front of a quaint home with a clothesline strung across the yard. Several colourful garments fluttered in the breeze. "We'll need to be quick and quiet," Mirabel whispered, her eyes darting about.

Harry cleared his throat. "I'll keep watch," he said. "The rest of you, grab what you need. And Milly? Be a dear and grab me something nice, won't you?"

Milly rolled her eyes, a flush creeping up her cheeks. She moved towards the clothesline, feeling yet another pang of guilt at the thought of stealing from an innocent ancient Alexandrian. Ashley and Fran seemed to share her unease.

"But... isn't this stealing?" Fran asked, looking uncomfortable. "Stealing is wrong." Milly silently agreed. She was also somewhat surprised, and relieved, that Fran hadn't picked up on the fact that they'd come here to *steal* from Alexander the Great's tomb in the first place. Fran was pretty intuitive, but Milly wasn't sure how closely she'd been paying attention to their conversations with Harry.

"Yeah, this doesn't feel right," Ashley added, her voice tinged with guilt.

Lucy, however, was already reaching for a tunic. "It's for the greater good," she said, likely trying to convince herself as much as her friends. "We need to blend in if we want to succeed, right?"

With a sense of reluctance and determination, Milly and the others began choosing garments that would help them blend in with the ancient Alexandrians. Just as they finished picking out clothes that fit them well enough, a voice called out from the nearby house. "What's going on out there?"

Panic surged through the group as they heard footsteps approaching. Mirabel quickly gestured for everyone to hide behind a nearby thicket, which, though small, would have to do. As the homeowner came closer, Mirabel stepped forward with a warm, charming smile. "Oh, hello there! We were just admiring your neighbour's lovely clothesline. Such beautiful garments!"

The homeowner eyed them suspiciously but seemed to soften at Mirabel's friendly demeanour. "Well, I suppose they *are* quite nice," she said, her tone lightening. "But what are you all doing here? And why are your companions hiding behind that bush?" She pointed at Milly and the others, who were crammed together like sardines behind the thicket. Louie, of course, barked loudly, completely giving away their already compromised position.

Mirabel quickly improvised. "You startled my companions," she said, gesturing to the others. "We're travellers passing through. We're not from around here, you see. And they're children, , please forgive them for being so curious about such lovely garments."

The homeowner seemed satisfied with the explanation and gave them a warm smile before waving them off. Once she was out of sight, Mirabel quickly plucked several garments from the clothesline and distributed them among the group. "I made sure to grab some smaller pieces of clothing for Fran and Charlie," she said. "Lucky for us, this person has children."

"We'll return the clothing when we're done exploring Alexander's tomb, right?" Fran asked, eyeing a small tunic and a child's skirt Mirabel had handed her.

"Of course," Mirabel reassured her. "And we probably won't be gone long. They probably won't even notice their clothes are missing."

"I hope not," Fran said, slipping the long skirt on over her own. "But what about Louie? What's he going to wear?" She smiled at the dog, who was currently lifting his leg next to the thicket.

Mirabel looked amused and folded her arms. "Louie's a dog. He doesn't need clothes. Though that lead of his is quite the giveaway." She gestured to Louie's colourful leash. "Most people around here let their dogs roam free. Do you think Louie could manage without his lead?"

"Uh, maybe..." Milly said, a little unsure. "I promised Mum I wouldn't lose him, though."

"Have some faith in him, Milly," Charlie piped up. "I don't know if you've noticed, but Louie's pretty obsessed with you. Even if he runs off for a bit, he'll come back."

Milly thought it over for a moment and then crouched down next to Louie. "Be a good boy, okay?" she said softly, scratching behind his ears before slowly unclipping his leash. To her surprise, Louie didn't dash off. He simply sat down beside her and let his tongue hang out happily. "That's a good boy," Milly said. "You just stay with me, Louie Roi. I'll keep you safe." She handed him one of his chews, much to his delight.

Louie barked and nuzzled his nose against Milly's knee, as if to confirm his loyalty.

4

JOURNEY TO THE UNDERWORLD

When they returned to Agnes's hut, the scene was a lively one. Agnes and Catalina were hunched over Milly's list of Persian symbols, comparing them with those they'd found in several dusty, old tomes scattered around the house. Faramund and Wolfstan were enthusiastically devouring the last of the loukoumades, and when Mirabel pushed open the door, they looked up with surprise, as though they had been caught in the act.

"Hey," Mirabel said, stifling a laugh. "Save some for the rest of us, would you?"

Wolfstan quickly swallowed and tried to conceal the empty plate behind his back. "There weren't that many left," he said, glancing at Faramund. "Right, Faramund?"

Faramund wiped crumbs from his moustache and chewed one last mouthful. "Mmhmm," he nodded, his voice muffled. "Delicious as always, Agnes!"

"I'm glad you enjoyed them, dears," Agnes replied, only half paying attention. She was peering through a magnifying glass at the fine print in a large tome. Her lips moved as she mumbled to herself, and though Milly could barely make out the words, she caught fragments: "Quest... Underworld... Nyx."

Agnes looked up suddenly, her eyes gleaming with excitement. "It seems that your journey to uncover the secrets of Alexander's tomb is far from over," she said cryptically. "To gain access to the tomb, you'll need to retrieve an agate from Nyx herself."

"Nyx?" Milly asked, glancing at her friends, puzzled. "Who's Nyx?"

"Who's Nyx?" Agnes echoed, her jaw nearly hitting the floor in disbelief. "What on earth are they teaching you in this future school of yours? Nyx is the goddess of the night, the daughter of Chaos and the mother of Thanatos. She resides in the Underworld and possesses untold mystical powers." Agnes beckoned Milly over to the tome. "This is Nyx." She pointed to an ancient illustration of a woman draped in black robes, her fingernails long and sharp as claws, and around her neck, a crude necklace of black agate.

"Oh," Milly said, her stomach sinking. "Uh... wow. How are we supposed to retrieve an agate from her? It has to be that one, doesn't it?" She pointed to the illustration of Nyx's necklace in the tome.

"That's correct," Agnes replied with a grim nod. "Once you retrieve the agate, you'll be able to use it to enter the tomb of Alexander. But..." She paused for a moment. "It's not going to be an easy journey. I can tell you that much."

Milly's heart raced at the thought of such a dangerous quest, but her resolve strengthened. "What do we need to do?"

Agnes leaned forward, her eyes intense. "You'll need to find my sister, Agatha. As I mentioned before, she guards the entrance to the Underworld with the gorgons. Tell her that Agnes sent you," she said with a smile. "If she takes a liking to you, she may even guide you further on your journey."

"Wow... the Underworld, huh?" Harry materialised beside Milly, peering over her shoulder at the illustration of Nyx. "I suppose we'll need weapons."

"I suppose you'll need companions," Wolfstan said, patting his bow. "What do you say, Captain? Mirabel? Faramund? Are you ready for another adventure?"

"Always," Faramund replied, patting his stomach and drawing his sword.

"Don't take that thing out in here!" Agnes snapped. "You'll put someone's eye out!"

Faramund sheepishly sheathed his sword again. "Where are we going to get weapons for the little ones?" he asked. "Should we head to the palace and stock up on supplies, or would it be better to travel light? It's up to you, Captain," he said, addressing Catalina.

Everyone turned to look at Catalina, who smiled boldly, twirling one of her throwing knives between her fingers. "We'll travel light for now," she said confidently. "I'm sure we'll find weapons along the way. The Underworld is a three-day trek from here, and we don't want Fran and Charlie getting worn out from carrying too much."

"This will no doubt be the toughest challenge we've faced yet," Mirabel said, raising an eyebrow. "As much as I admire your carefree spirit, Catalina, we should make sure we're prepared."

"We've got our weapons ready," Catalina replied, tucking her throwing knife back into her boot. "I see no reason to burden the children with weapons right now, especially when we can protect them. From what I've heard, this journey won't become particularly perilous until the third day, so we'll have time to 'prepare,' as you put it, along the way."

"Hmph." Mirabel crossed her arms, clearly irritated, but shrugged. "Okay, then. Don't say I didn't warn you."

"Always the cautious one, Mirabel," Faramund teased.

"I prefer to think of myself as the smart one." Mirabel gave Ashley a knowing smile and flicked her hair over her shoulder. "Well, then. What are we waiting for? We should try to cover as much ground as we can before nightfall. Ashley, you're with me. Have you been working on your swordsmanship?"

"I haven't had time," Ashley admitted. "I was planning on joining the fencing club at school, but…" The two of them continued chatting as Catalina and Agnes exchanged farewells.

"Good luck, dears," Agnes said warmly, wrapping Catalina in a tight hug. "And good luck, children! Say 'hello' to my sister for me!"

After leaving Agnes's hut, Catalina, with Milly and Louie in tow, began leading the way to the Underworld. But not before stopping in Alexandria for supplies. "Personally, I prefer to sleep under the stars on the cold, hard ground like a true warrior," Catalina remarked with a sideways glance at Mirabel. "But some of us can't manage without a soft bed and enough food to feed the Lernean Hydra, and that thing had an infinite number of heads! Remember when we fought the Lernean Hydra, Wolfstan?" She looked back at him, but he was too busy talking to Harry about archery.

"How could I forget?" Wolfstan replied with a chuckle. "When you cut off one of the Lernean Hydra's many heads, two more grow back in its place," he explained to Harry. "No, thank you! I'll leave slaying that particular beast to Hercules!"

"Hercules is real?" Charlie asked, his eyes wide with excitement.

"Certainly," Faramund said with a grin. "I imagine in your time, he's merely a legend. We've never met him, but he's as real as the ground we're standing on."

"So, you didn't manage to kill it?" Harry asked eagerly, looking at Wolfstan with a sense of curiosity.

"Oh, goodness no," Wolfstan replied. "We ran into the Lernean Hydra by accident a long time ago. It was meant to be a simple mission, escorting the princess of Faramund's kingdom back home after she ran away." He shrugged. "But, alas... nothing is ever simple."

"You can say that again," Mirabel muttered, still giving Catalina the cold shoulder as they made their way into the heart of Alexandria. "How much money do you have left, Faramund?"

Faramund pulled out a small cloth bag and peered inside. "Not much," he said with a sigh. "But it should be enough to buy some blankets and rations for a day or two." He looked around at the group. "We've, uh, kind of got a lot of mouths to feed."

"We brought food!" Milly said, patting her bookbag. "Mum packed us sandwiches. We'll make them last so you don't have to worry about feeding us." She glanced around, feeling a bit self-conscious. The last thing she wanted was to be a burden on her fellow adventurers. She also wondered if they secretly resented her for bringing so many people along , not to mention a dog. But as far as she was concerned, Louie, her friends, and her siblings were a package deal.

"Nonsense," Mirabel said with a grin. "We'll feed you. My main concern, though, is the little ones," she said, glancing at Fran and Charlie. "Will you two be alright? We don't have much money for food, and the journey to the Underworld is long and dangerous,"

"We can handle it," Fran replied confidently, looking up at Charlie. "Right, Charlie? We're tough."

"Yeah!" Charlie agreed, though Milly could see the faint hint of exhaustion already creeping into his expression. "I want to go on an adventure!"

"Very well," Mirabel said, smiling warmly. "Milly and Harry will be in charge of looking after the little ones, then. Not that you two can't hold your own, but, "

"We'll look after them, Mirabel," Milly said, placing a reassuring hand on her sister's shoulder. "Don't worry. I'd never let anything happen to my siblings."

Mirabel nodded and stayed with them while Faramund, Wolfstan, and Catalina gathered blankets and food rations from nearby merchants. "We'll probably get a chance to... er... acquire more money along the way," Mirabel said, casting a glance toward the others. "Maybe Catalina's right. I do worry too much sometimes."

"There's nothing wrong with being prepared," Ashley told her. "Though, there does seem to be a bit of tension between you and Catalina. Are you two not getting along lately?"

Mirabel sighed. "Oh, we fight like sisters. We all get on each other's nerves now and then. You'll probably see it soon enough. That's what happens when you spend so much time together. No one knows how to drive you mad quite like your friends." She flashed a smile at Milly, Fran, and Charlie. "Especially siblings. You three will have to work hard if you want to avoid throttling each other on this trip."

"I fight with Lucy all the time," Fran said, giving Milly a pointed look. "But we always make up in the end."

Mirabel laughed. "Well, that's good to hear."

"Yeah, and sometimes I get annoyed with Milly," Lucy added with a playful sneer, "but only when she talks non-stop about, "

"Lucy!" Milly interrupted, her face turning crimson. She shot a quick glance at Harry, hoping he hadn't caught the implication. She quickly turned her attention to Catalina, Faramund, and Wolfstan shopping for supplies, hoping to distract herself from the conversation. Harry, ever oblivious, seemed completely unaware of the tension, and Milly silently thanked him for it.

After some time, Catalina and the others returned with their purchases. Milly, Ashley, Lucy, and Harry offered to carry some of the rations so the load wouldn't fall entirely on the others. "Thanks," Catalina said, brushing her hands together. "Well, we'd better get moving. The Underworld is a long way off."

The journey took them through rolling hills, dotted with olive groves. The silver-green leaves shimmered in the sunlight, and the air was fragrant with wildflowers, vibrant yellow and violet blossoms lining the edges of their winding path. In the distance, the soothing sound of a river babbled softly, and towering cypress trees stood like sentinels against the bright, cloudless sky.

As they walked, Catalina and Wolfstan kept Fran and Charlie entertained with stories of their past. Catalina shared tales of monster-slaying adventures, while Wolfstan recounted his encounters with gods and goddesses. Harry, with Charlie riding piggyback on his shoulders, listened intently.

"Are you sure you're not embellishing, Wolfstan?" Harry asked, raising an eyebrow after Wolfstan told them of Aphrodite, the goddess of beauty, asking for his hand in marriage.

"Certainly not!" Wolfstan declared, puffing his chest out. "Faramund can back me up."

"I never said that," Faramund interjected, clearly enjoying the banter.

"Aphrodite was in love with me," Wolfstan continued, shooting a playful glare at Faramund. "But I told her, 'My heart belongs to my wife.' Well, the goddess wasn't too happy about that. I'd probably still be her prisoner if Catalina and the others hadn't come to my rescue." Louie barked as if in response, running circles around him as though calling him out on his embellishments.

Mirabel rolled her eyes. "Do you always have to make up stories, Wolfstan?" she asked, giving him a gentle shove.

"Yeah, as if the goddess of beauty would fancy you," Faramund added with a chuckle.

Milly, Fran, Ashley, and Lucy walked behind, laughing at Wolfstan's tall tale, their surroundings shifting as the landscape grew more rugged and mysterious. The sun began to dip below the horizon, casting a warm, golden glow over the group. The air was rich with the scent of wild herbs, carried on a cool breeze that rustled through the trees.

As night approached, the terrain became even more foreboding. Massive boulders loomed overhead, their surfaces covered in thick moss and lichen. The temperature dropped, and the sky darkened further as they came upon an ancient ruin, its half-crumbled walls offering shelter for the night.

"We'll be safe here," Mirabel said, setting down her bag and unrolling one of the blankets. "Who wants to help me make dinner?" She rummaged through Faramund's bag, pulling out a loaf of bread, some wrapped lamb, and a few pieces of fruit. "Hmm... maybe we should save the meat for later. We'll need it for the return trip, after all,"

"It'll spoil if we don't eat it now," Faramund said with a grin. "Come on, why not have a nice meal on our first night out here?" He grabbed the lamb and began collecting kindling for a fire. "Roasted lamb and bread with pomegranate jam sounds like heaven right now."

Milly's stomach rumbled in agreement. She was exhausted from the long walk and, despite her earlier promise to her friends that the sandwiches would suffice, the thought of a proper meal was too tempting to ignore. Louie seemed to feel the same way, licking his lips in anticipation. Faramund quickly realised that , if he left the lamb unattended, Louie would devour it in seconds. So, he handed the meat to Milly, who wrinkled her nose as the juices leaked from the leaves and soaked into her hands.

Perhaps a ham sandwich wouldn't be so bad after all, Milly thought with a grimace.

As Catalina, Mirabel, Faramund, and the others worked together to prepare the camp, Louie whimpered, hopping up on Milly and barking eagerly. "No, Louie," Milly said, holding the lamb meat high out of his reach. "You'll get some in a bit, but you have to be patient."

"Want me to hold that for you?" Harry asked, noticing Milly's struggle as he added kindling to the fire that Wolfstan was stoking.

"Uh, sure," Milly said gratefully, handing him the leaf-wrapped lamb. "I like eating meat, but not handling it. And Louie's being a pain, of course."

"Oh, he can't help it," Harry said, giving Louie an affectionate scratch behind the ear. "There might be a stream nearby if you want to wash your hands. I could've sworn I heard water while we were walking."

"The Acheron River," Wolfstan nodded. "It's up that way." He pointed vaguely with a stick. "But don't go alone. Harry, why don't you go with Milly? Take Faramund's sword with you. You never know what's lurking around here, especially at night. I'll keep an eye on the meat."

Harry's eyes brightened. "Alright," he said, eagerly picking up Faramund's sword.

"I'm not sure I trust you to watch the meat on your own, Wolfstan," Mirabel said, appearing just as Fran, Ashley, and the others returned with , firewood. "We've gathered enough wood now, so I'll help with the fire."

"Very well," Wolfstan said, looking mildly disappointed as Harry took the lamb meat from him. "Would you care to help me prepare some lamb skewers, Mirabel? We'll need to heat the bread and open up a pomegranate."

"I'll take care of the pomegranate," Mirabel said, placing it on a flat rock and drawing her sword to slice it open.

Fran, who had dropped her bundle of firewood near Wolfstan, walked up to Milly and Harry with a sweet smile. "Are you going somewhere?" she asked. "Can I come with you?"

"Uh…" Milly hesitated, a little irritated that her moment alone with Harry was being interrupted. "I'm just going to the river to wash my hands. It's not that exciting."

"Take this torch," Mirabel said, dipping a large, moss-covered branch into the fire and handing it to Harry. "If you could bring back some water, too, that would be great. There's a pot in my bag; you can fill it up, and purify it over the fire."

"Sure!" Milly said, happy to be of help. She dug through Mirabel's bag, pulled out the small cooking pot, and set off with Harry and Fran toward the Acheron River.

The trio made their way to the water's edge, Harry swinging Faramund's sword almost carelessly through the tall grass that lined the trail. Milly found the soft murmur of the babbling river soothing and was grateful for the chance to dip her sticky hands into the crystal-clear water. Harry crouched down next to her, holding the torch near her hands so that she could see what she was doing.

"Thanks," Milly said, shaking her hands dry and taking the torch from him. "I can hold onto this now."

She glanced at Faramund's sword. "Looks like your hands are full."

"Sure," Harry replied, shrugging as he handed the torch to Milly. They sat by the river for a few minutes, savouring the serene beauty of the moonlight glistening on the calm water, while Fran filled Mirabel's cooking pot nearby.

"Milly... I wanted to talk to you about something," Harry said, absentmindedly sticking the tip of Faramund's sword into the mud.

Milly's heart skipped a beat. "Of course," she said, trying to keep her voice steady. "What's up?"

Just then, Fran squealed from the river's edge. Jumping up and down and pointing excitedly, she cried, "Look! Over there!"

Milly and Harry turned to see what Fran was pointing at, their eyes widening in astonishment. A unicorn, its coat shimmering in hues of silver and gold, stood gracefully at the water's edge. Its mane, a cascade of iridescent colours, floated gently in the breeze as it drank from the crystal-clear stream.

The unicorn's horn, spiralling majestically, caught the moonlight and refracted it into a dazzling display of colours. Its eyes, gentle, yet, wary, met theirs with an air of quiet curiosity.

Milly and Harry exchanged incredulous looks, marvelling at the sight before them. Fran's face lit up with pure joy as she watched the mythical creature in awe. "It's a unicorn," she whispered, her voice filled with wonder.

Milly beamed at Harry. This was like a dream come true for Fran, who'd only ever read about unicorns in storybooks. She placed her hands on Fran's shoulders, and the two of them watched, mouths agape, as the unicorn bent down to drink from the river once more.

"I can't believe it," Milly said, keeping her voice low to avoid startling the creature. "Good eye, Fran."

"I can't wait to tell Mum," Fran said, practically bouncing with excitement. "I wish I could take a picture," she added in a whisper.

"I wonder if it means something," Harry said, eyeing the unicorn thoughtfully. "Seeing a unicorn has to be rare, even in a world like this."

Milly nodded, making a mental note to ask Mirabel about it when they returned to camp. All three of them felt perfectly content to continue watching the majestic creature, but the moment was suddenly shattered by a sharp disturbance. An arrow whistled through the air and struck the unicorn's leg with a sickening thud. The creature let out a cry of pain and stumbled over a tree root before collapsing to the ground. Fran's joyful expression immediately morphed into one of shock and horror. Without thinking, she waded into the river, her heart swelling with compassion and a desperate need to help the wounded unicorn.

"Fran, wait!" Milly shouted, grabbing her by the elbow before she could get any further into the dark water. "I don't know how deep the water is in the middle! It might be dangerous!"

Fran was too distraught to listen, thrashing against Milly's grasp. "I can swim!" she snapped, attempting to pull away. "Let go of me!"

Milly exchanged a worried glance with Harry before following Fran into the water. They struggled against the current, their clothes quickly soaking through. The shock of the coldness of the water caught them both off guard.

"My God!" Harry exclaimed. "It's freezing!"

"That's the least of our worries," Milly replied. "Come on. We have to catch up with Fran before whoever, or whatever, shot that arrow reaches her first."

Fran knelt by the riverbank, her hands trembling as she gently removed the arrow from the unicorn's leg. The unicorn whimpered, its eyes clouded with pain and confusion. "It's okay," Fran whispered, her voice quivering with emotion. "We're here to help you."

Milly and Harry crouched down beside Fran, their hearts heavy with concern for the creature. Up close, the unicorn was even more breathtaking than they had imagined. Its coat shimmered with iridescent silver, reflecting the dappled moonlight that filtered through the trees. Each strand of its mane and tail seemed to sway with the wind, and its eyes, large and expressive, glistened with a blend of intelligence and magic.

Its horn, spiralling gracefully from its forehead, was flawless and gleaming, glowing softly in the moonlight. Despite its pain, the unicorn remained remarkably calm and trusting as Fran stroked its lustrous mane. "We'll help you get better," Fran promised, her eyes locked with the unicorn's. "You're safe now."

The unicorn gave a soft whinny, as though understanding her words. Its breathing gradually slowed, and the tension in its muscles began to ease.

Then, to Milly's surprise, Fran pressed her hand over the unicorn's wound. She closed her eyes, concentrating deeply as though trying to focus. Milly frowned, unsure of what Fran was attempting. What is she doing? Milly wondered. And then it clicked. Fran was trying to heal the unicorn.

"Fran," Milly said softly, her voice strained with concern. "We have to get help. You don't even know if you have healing powers!"

"I have to try," Fran said, her fingers now stained with the silver liquid that leaked from the unicorn's wound. Unicorn blood, Milly thought with a grimace.

Fran closed her eyes once more, focusing with all her might on the injury. But after a few moments, nothing happened, and Fran's face crumpled in frustration as tears welled up in her eyes. "Come on!" she cried. "Mum can heal things! Why can't I?"

Harry, meanwhile, was watching the scene with a perplexed expression. "Your mum has healing powers?" he asked, looking slightly incredulous.

Milly sighed and ran a hand through her hair, feeling a bit overwhelmed by everything. "It's a long story," she said. "Mum's a descendant of Athena, so she has powers. She told us that me, Fran, and Charlie might have powers too, but, um..." She shared a look of quiet desperation with Fran. "We haven't discovered them yet."

"Powers?" Harry scratched his head, clearly baffled. He almost looked like he didn't believe her, but Milly couldn't blame him. "What sort of powers? Healing powers, or-"

"We're not sure," Milly said, cutting him off when she heard rustling in the nearby bushes. "We'll talk about it later, okay?"

Just then, none other than Wolfstan burst out of the bushes, his bow and quiver of arrows slung over his shoulder. He was followed closely by Catalina and Louie.

"Get away from that thing!" Catalina shouted, rushing forward to grab Fran and drag her away from the unicorn. "I know it looks beautiful, but it's dangerous!"

Louie, standing guard beside Catalina, barked menacingly at the unicorn, baring his teeth.

Fran kicked and screamed, trying to break free from Catalina's grasp. She kneed her in the stomach and flopped out of her arms, immediately crawling back to the unicorn. To Milly's surprise, Fran threw herself over the unicorn's body, shielding it with her own. "You did this!" she shouted at Wolfstan, her voice thick with anger. "How could you hurt such an innocent creature?"

"Please try to calm down, Fran," Catalina said, massaging her stomach where Fran had kneed her. "I know it looks bad, but if Wolfstan hadn't shot the unicorn, it would have,"

"I don't care!" Fran shouted, her tears streaming down her face as she buried her face in the unicorn's soft mane. Milly moved to comfort her, but Fran shoved her away. "Don't touch me! Leave me alone!"

"Fran..." Milly said, her voice soft with sympathy. "There has to be a good reason why Wolfstan shot the unicorn." She looked at Wolfstan, hoping for some explanation. "Why did you shoot it?" she asked, before turning to Catalina. "What do you mean by 'it's dangerous'?"

"The unicorn is a remarkable creature," Catalina said, her eyes deliberately avoiding the unicorn. She shielded her face with her hand as she spoke to Milly. Wolfstan did the same, clearly uncomfortable. "You see, the unicorn is so beautiful that those who gaze upon it long enough are compelled to follow it, no matter where it leads. It's a simple enchantment, but it's still dangerous. Fran has been enchanted. She won't be able to think about anything other than the unicorn now. She won't be able to eat, drink, or sleep. That's why Wolfstan shot it, to prevent it from running off and taking you all with it."

"You're lying!" Fran spat, her face flushed with fury. But Milly wasn't so sure. Catalina's tone was serious, and there was a note of truth in her words that Milly couldn't ignore. Even Louie seemed to realise this, as he tugged gently at the back of Fran's tunic with his teeth.

"I don't think she is, Fran," Milly said softly, gently guiding her sister away from the unicorn. "Come on, we should get back to camp."

"I'm not going anywhere," Fran said, clinging to the unicorn's neck. "She needs my help."

"She?" Harry asked, tilting his head in confusion. "Um... I'm pretty sure the unicorn's a boy."

Fran looked up, her face streaked with tears. "What do you mean? All unicorns are girls."

"Well, never mind that," Wolfstan said, his cheeks flushed. "The unicorn will be fine, Fran. I didn't mean to kill it. He'll, uh, she'll heal quickly. Look." He pointed at the unicorn's wound, which was already starting to close. Moments later, the creature stood up and gave a loud whinny before darting into the deep, dark woods. Louie barked furiously at it but, to Milly's surprise, didn't chase after it.

"See?" Wolfstan said with a hopeful grin.

"No!" Fran cried, scrambling through the bushes after the unicorn. Her skirt caught on a gnarled branch, and she yelped in frustration. "Come back! I can't live without you!"

Catalina sighed, rolling her eyes, before lifting Fran over her shoulder like a sack of potatoes.

"Put me down!" Fran yelled, kicking and flailing in Catalina's grip. "I want to go with the unicorn!"

"Alright then," Catalina said, letting out a small sigh as she smiled at Milly and Harry. "Let's get back to camp."

5

THE CYCLOPS'S RIDDLE

It was Fran's turn to ride on Harry's shoulders as they trekked through the mountainous landscape the following day. She had refused to eat dinner the night before, as well as breakfast that morning, leaving her more than a little tired and irritable. Louie trailed behind them, whimpering occasionally out of concern for Fran. Milly shared similar feelings. Mirabel had assured Milly that creating an antidote for the unicorn's enchantment would be, straightforward, provided they could find the necessary ingredients. "We'll need a sprig of sage, a touch of saffron, and a bit of chamomile. Do you fancy chamomile tea, Fran?"

Fran didn't respond. She sat atop Harry's shoulders, her expression blank. Catalina had informed Milly that her sister would remain rather despondent until they administered the antidote. At least she was no longer kicking and screaming. Milly felt a pang of sympathy for her. She had hoped that encountering a unicorn would be a magical experience for Fran, but it had turned out to be sad and stressful instead. She still felt a flicker of anger towards Wolfstan for shooting the unicorn in front of her little sister, but she understood he was merely trying to protect them.

Mirabel offered Milly a sad smile. "We'll be able to find all the herbs we need out here," she said. "Just keep your eyes peeled."

"Right," Milly replied, scanning the ground as she walked, despite not knowing what saffron or chamomile looked like. She was beginning to miss her mother terribly, even though she had seen her just the day before. Mum would know exactly what to do in this situation, she thought. She would hold Fran in her arms and know precisely what to say to make her feel better. Shaking the thought from her mind, she focused on the task at hand. Their mother trusted them to embark on this adventure together, and she particularly trusted Milly to protect Fran and Charlie. "I can do this," she muttered. "It's going to be okay." Just then, she felt something soft brush against her fingers and looked down to see Harry grasping her hand. He gave it a gentle squeeze before letting go, prompting a smile from her.

"I found some saffron!" Faramund announced, kneeling to pluck it from a patch of grass. "Are you planning on making tea for all of us, Mirabel? That would be très magnifique!"

"I suppose," Mirabel replied. "Good work, Faramund. It shouldn't be too difficult to find the chamomile and sage now..."

After another hour or so of searching, the group had gathered everything they needed to concoct the antidote for Fran. Mirabel set up her cooking pot, , still filled with the water Fran had scooped from the river the night before, , and asked Wolfstan and Faramund to start a fire. Ashley and Lucy sat on either side of Milly around the cooking pot while the others collected kindling. Louie continued to fuss over Fran, licking her face and nudging her with his nose, but she remained unresponsive.

"I can't believe you saw a real live unicorn," Lucy said. "I must admit, I'm a bit jealous."

"You shouldn't be," Mirabel replied, breaking up the herbs in her cooking pot. "My mother passed away because she was enchanted by a unicorn, you know." The others stared at her, expressions of slight horror on their faces. "It happened a long time ago," she added. "But still. Catalina wasn't lying to you, Milly. Unicorns are dangerous."

"I understand that now," Milly said. "It's just... surprising. And sad. Fran was so excited."

"I would have been excited too," Ashley said. "I loved unicorns when I was a little girl."

"You're still a little girl," Wolfstan remarked, setting down a pile of firewood next to Mirabel and taking a seat directly across from them. "There are far too many little girls on this journey." Then, noticing the looks on Milly, Ashley, and Lucy's faces, he smiled nervously. "Only joking," he added.

"Right," Milly said, rolling her eyes. "Are you almost done with the antidote, Mirabel? I'm worried about Fran."

"It's almost finished," Mirabel said, stirring the hot water and herbs in the cooking pot with a large stick. "She'll be back to her normal self a few minutes after drinking it, so don't fret."

"You'll have to force it down my throat," Fran mumbled under her breath. "I don't want to stop thinking about that unicorn. Not ever."

"I know, Fran," Milly said. "But you must understand... you're under the unicorn's spell. If you don't drink this tea, you might..." She paused, taking a sharp breath, unable to bring herself to finish the thought. "You might get hurt badly."

"I don't care," Fran replied, her tone completely deadpan. Louie whimpered and nudged her with his nose again, but she ignored him. "I wanted to go with the unicorn, and you wouldn't let me." She glared at Milly. "I'll never forget that."

"It's done," Mirabel announced as the remaining members of the group joined them around the cooking pot. "We can take turns drinking from the pot, but first things first," she fixed Fran with a determined look. "We've got to make sure that you take your medicine, don't we?"

"No!" Fran shouted. "You can't make me!" She clamped her mouth shut and covered her face with her hands.

Milly couldn't help but grin. She felt guilty for finding the situation amusing, but it was just like when their mum tried to get Fran to take medicine at home. "Come on then, Fran," she said. "Don't be a baby."

"You're just like Louie," Charlie said, giggling a little. "Good thing it's not a pill, or we'd have to hide it in a piece of cheese for you."

"Shut up!" Fran retorted, fresh tears springing to her eyes. "I don't want to! I don't want to! I don't want," Just then, Mirabel cupped some warm tea in her hand and quickly brought it to Fran's lips. She held Fran's mouth open with her fingers as Fran struggled, eventually managing to trickle the tea down her throat. Fran reluctantly swallowed and then scraped her tongue with her fingers. "You've poisoned me!" she shouted. "How dare you?"

"Oh, hush," Mirabel said. "It doesn't taste that bad, does it? Just give it a minute, Fran. You'll feel better soon." The rest of them took turns drinking from the cooking pot while Fran sulked. Sure enough, a few minutes later, she was asking if she could have some more.

"Of course," Mirabel said, handing Fran the cooking pot. "Perhaps you're feeling hungry too?"

"Yeah..." Fran said, still a bit dazed. "I'm really hungry. Milly? Can I have my sandwich now?"

"Sure, Fran," Milly replied, silently thanking Mirabel as she rummaged through her bag. She quickly found one of the brown bag lunches their mother had packed for them and handed it to her sister. "You want one too, Charlie?"

Charlie nodded. They ate sandwiches and drank tea in silence for a while until Catalina announced it was time to start walking again. "Come on, everyone," she said, standing up and brushing some dirt off her tunic. "This journey is far from over. We've still got a long way to go." After packing up their lunches and extinguishing the fire, they set off towards the rugged mountain ridges, which seemed to carve into the horizon like blades. Milly wondered what challenges lay ahead and began contemplating how she would explain to Harry, Ashley, and Lucy the potential power that lay dormant within her.

The sun beat down on the backs of their necks, and Milly had lost track of how long they'd been walking. Three hours? Four? It didn't matter. She was beginning to feel delirious, and her siblings and friends didn't seem to be faring particularly well either, from what she could tell. Nobody dared to complain, though. Each of them had chosen to embark on this adventure, and once again, the last thing Milly wanted was to be a burden to Catalina and the others. Even Charlie had decided to walk on his own, , now holding Harry's hand instead of riding on his shoulders. He wore a determined expression, and despite frequently tripping over tree roots, he didn't stop walking.

"Are you doing okay, Charlie?" Milly asked him.

"Never... better..." Charlie panted.

Milly smiled, but she couldn't shake the worry for her younger siblings. "What about you, Fran?"

"I'm okay," Fran replied. "Remember that time we got lost with Mum and Dad while hiking the Rùm Cuillin trail during that camping trip? It's just like that."

"I suppose you're right," Milly said, admiring her sister's resilience.

"Except we're not lost," Catalina interjected, wiping sweat from her brow. "I know exactly where we're going."

"I sure hope so," Mirabel said. "Have you ever been to the Underworld before, Catalina? Are you sure you know the way?"

"Doubting me again, are you, Mirabel?" Catalina shot her a miffed look. "No, I've never been to the Underworld, but I studied the map at Agnes's house before we left. You don't have anything to worry about."

"Why didn't you bring the map with you?" Mirabel asked.

"I'm not going to lug around an enormous tome," Catalina replied. "And Agnes wasn't about to let me rip the page out. Anyway, like I said, we'll be fine. I'm fairly sure we're going the right way."

"'Fairly sure?'" Faramund scoffed. "Alright then. I suppose I have no choice but to trust your judgement, Captain. But if it turns out we've been going in the wrong direction this whole time, "

"There!" Catalina's face lit up. She pointed to a large wooden bridge in the distance. "As you can all see," she gestured towards the roaring Acheron River nearby, "the river's been rough, so we haven't been able to cross it. That bridge is exactly where we're supposed to cross to get to the path that leads to the Underworld!" She surveyed everyone's tired faces. "After we cross, we'll take a break," she promised.

They made their way towards the bridge, Charlie finally accepting a ride on Harry's shoulders and Fran holding Milly's hand. "Hey, Milly? Um..." Fran stammered. "I've been meaning to tell you about something. Now that I've got my head on straight again, I've been thinking about what happened with the unicorn, "

"Try not to think about that, Fran," Milly cautioned. "You'll make yourself sick again, "

"No, I'm okay," Fran insisted, squeezing Milly's hand. "It's just... when I was petting the unicorn and comforting her... I could, um... understand what she was thinking. It was as if she was speaking to me with her thoughts. She said, 'Help me, child... please help me.' It just about broke my heart."

Milly halted in her tracks. "What do you mean she was 'speaking to you with her thoughts'? Were you able to hear her thoughts, or do you think you were just imagining it, "

"I wasn't imagining anything," Fran replied patiently. "I think maybe... that's my power. I can speak to animals, or at least understand them on a deeper level. I'm not sure how I did it, though." She released Milly's hand and examined her own fingers.

"Maybe it's because I was touching the unicorn while talking to her. Perhaps unicorns are somewhat telepathic."

"They're not," Catalina interjected, glancing back at them. "At least... not that I know of. You should try speaking to Louie, Fran. If you can communicate with animals, then you should be able to understand what he's thinking, right?"

Fran looked at Louie, who was happily trotting alongside them with his tongue lolling out. "Well, I wouldn't be able to prove that I know what he's thinking, would I?" she said, her cheeks flushing. "And... and... I don't even know how to use this power yet." Fran continued to gaze at Louie, wringing her hands.

"Dream on, Fran," Charlie said, a sceptical smile tugging at his lips. "Mum said we're probably too young to discover our powers, remember? You're probably still a bit woozy from being under the unicorn's spell, I reckon."

"What's this about powers?" Lucy asked, jogging to catch up with Milly, Fran, Charlie, and Harry. "Do you have powers, Milly?" She burst into laughter, clutching her stomach, tears welling up in her eyes. "Oh, please!" she managed between laughs. "That's too good!"

"Pipe down, Lucy," Harry said, frowning. "Milly, Fran, and Charlie are descendants of a powerful goddess, aren't they?" He glanced at Milly, as though looking for confirmation.

Milly nodded. "It makes sense that they would have powers," she said, trying to reassure the group.

"Thank you, Harry," Milly said. They were about ten paces away from the great wooden bridge when she heard a deep, rumbling sound, followed by the earth trembling beneath her feet. "What was that?" she asked, instinctively stepping in front of Fran, Charlie, and Louie to protect them. "Please tell me you heard that."

Wolfstan had already drawn his bow, ready for anything. "Get behind us, children," he ordered. "And no sudden movements."

As Milly and the others huddled together, a towering figure emerged from the thick forest at the far end of the bridge. It was a Cyclops. Its enormous single eye scanned its surroundings, and, upon spotting them, , it let out a mighty growl. The creature stomped closer, each step shaking the ground. Milly's heart raced as she tried to think of a plan. She glanced at Catalina, Faramund, and Mirabel, all of whom were drawing their weapons.

With a deep, rumbling voice, the Cyclops spoke. "What business do you have here? Who dares to cross my bridge?"

Catalina cleared her throat, her throwing knives already poised in her hands. "We mean no harm, Cyclops," she said firmly. "We only seek passage to the Underworld. We have important business there."

The Cyclops narrowed his enormous eye, scrutinising the group. "Hmm, very well," he said, his voice dark and low. "But first, you must answer my riddle. Only the worthy may cross my bridge."

Catalina exchanged a quick, nervous glance with Mirabel. Riddles weren't her strong point, but there was no other option. "Speak your riddle," she said, trying to sound more confident than she felt.

Milly could see Catalina was forcing herself to appear calm. Even she could tell that the woman was uneasy.

"Why don't we just end this now?" Wolfstan muttered, his hand tightening on his bowstring. "If I blind him, we'll be able to cross the bridge... just as long as we're quiet."

"Hold on, Wolfstan," Mirabel said quickly. "We shouldn't do anything rash. We're travelling with children, remember?"

Wolfstan shot her an irritated glance before lowering his bow. "Fine," he said reluctantly. "Let's hear the riddle, then." His eyes never left the Cyclops.

The Cyclops grinned, showing rows of jagged teeth. "I will either grill you or boil you," he said. "If you're right, I will grill you. If you're wrong, I will boil you."

"He's going to eat us!" Charlie screamed, gripping Milly's arm in panic. She tried to soothe him, but her own nerves were on edge as well. Meanwhile, Catalina and Mirabel kept the Cyclops distracted, bombarding him with questions.

"That's not much of a riddle, is it?" Catalina demanded, brandishing one of her throwing knives. "Give us a proper riddle, Cyclops, or we'll blind you."

Mirabel appeared deep in thought, her brow furrowed. "Wait a minute," she said, grabbing Catalina by the wrist. "It is a riddle, but we need to think carefully about how we answer it. Will you give us some time to think, Cyclops?"

The Cyclops tilted his head, blinking slowly at them. "Take all the time you need," he said with a wicked grin. "It's been ages since anyone answered my riddle correctly. The last man who tried to cross my bridge was a hero, though... and you're nothing of the sort." He laughed, clutching his massive belly. "I wish you luck," he said. "You'll need it."

"Wretched beast," Wolfstan muttered under his breath. "Well then, Mirabel... what do you think?"

Mirabel repeated the Cyclops's riddle aloud. "'I will either grill you or boil you,'" she murmured, frowning. "'If you're right, I will grill you. If you're wrong, I will boil you.'" She tapped her chin thoughtfully. "Hmm..."

She turned to Ashley. "What do you think, Ashley? You're good with riddles, aren't you?"

Ashley stood silently, her arms folded across her chest, lost in thought. Milly, couldn't help but notice her usual lack of confidence. "Um..." Ashley began, "I think... unless we're allowed to ask questions, it's just a guessing game. I'm not sure we have a good chance of figuring this out." She ran a hand through her hair, exhaling heavily. "This is a mess."

Milly glanced up at the sky, then down at Louie, who was sitting at her feet. She scratched him behind the ears and handed him a Louie chewie as she pondered their predicament. "How are we supposed to know whether he's going to boil or grill us?" she murmured.

"I don't want him doing either of those things!" Fran wailed. "Maybe we should come back later..."

"No," Catalina said firmly. "We've come too far." She cleared her throat and addressed the Cyclops again. "Guardian of the bridge," she said, her voice steady, "may we ask you some questions before we answer your riddle?"

The Cyclops smiled in amusement. "Certainly," he said, his deep voice rumbling. "But I can't promise I'll give you the answers you seek."

Catalina pursed her lips, thinking quickly. "One moment," she said. Turning to the others, she spoke in a low voice. "We need to do some reconnaissance."

"Reconna-what?" Charlie asked, furrowing his brow.

"It means we need to sneak around and gather clues," Lucy explained, glancing at Catalina. "Right?"

Catalina shrugged. "Pretty much," she said. "A few of us will stay here to distract him while a small group checks out his cave." She pointed to a large cave just a short distance from the bridge. "Faramund, I'll have you lead that group. Look around the Cyclops's lair and see if you can figure out whether he's planning to boil or grill us."

Faramund blinked, his expression blank. "How am I supposed to do that?"

Catalina sighed patiently. "Well, if he has a large cooking pot, he's likely to boil us. If there's a fire pit and several large sticks, he probably plans to grill us."

"Oh," Faramund said slowly, still looking unsure. "What if he has both?"

Catalina threw her hands up in exasperation. "Just figure it out!" she said. "I know you can do

it, Faramund."

Faramund gave a firm nod, then turned to the group. "Alright," he said. "You four are with me." He gestured to Wolfstan, Milly, Ashley, and Louie. Louie yapped excitedly and began running in circles around him. "We need to stay quiet, though," Faramund added in a whisper, shooting Louie a pointed look. "Catalina and the others, will keep him distracted. Cyclops aren't very clever, you see," he said, glancing over at the creature, who was using an olive branch to floss between his giant toes. "But still, we need to stay out of sight."

Milly crouched down beside Louie, giving him a gentle shush. "We have to be quiet, boy," she whispered, stroking his fur. "You're going to help us figure out the Cyclops's riddle, right?" Louie gave a little whine but licked her hand, clearly understanding the task.

Faramund looked at them seriously. "I want to bring Louie along for his sense of smell. Maybe he'll notice something we don't. Alright," he said, nodding towards Catalina and Mirabel. "You'd better distract him well. I'd rather not be boiled."

With that, Catalina and Mirabel took a few cautious steps towards the Cyclops, preparing to entertain him with whatever distraction they could muster. Meanwhile, Faramund led the small group into the dense forest surrounding the Cyclops's cave. The air smelled of pine needles and damp earth as they moved carefully through the underbrush. Louie's nose twitched, picking up all manner of scents.

After what seemed like an age, they finally reached the entrance to the cave. It loomed darkly before them, , a gaping maw that seemed to swallow the weak light filtering through the trees. Faramund gestured for them to stay close as they stepped inside. As their footsteps echoed off the rocky walls, Milly's heart hammered in her chest. They ventured deeper into the gloom, with Wolfstan lighting a torch.

The, cave stank, and Milly wrinkled her nose in disgust. Bones lay piled in one corner, likely the remains of the Cyclops's meals. Crude tools were scattered haphazardly around the floor. "Keep it together," Milly whispered to herself, exchanging anxious glances with Ashley.

She sent Louie over to sniff the rotting bones in the corner. He didn't seem too enthusiastic. But then, Milly's eyes landed on a large cooking pot near the centre of the cave. Steam rose from it, carrying an awful stench. She covered her nose, fighting back nausea as she moved closer.

Next to the pot was a worn book, its pages dog-eared and stained. Milly flipped through it, scanning the strange symbols and diagrams. Then she found it: a page marked with greasy fingerprints, detailing the process of boiling chicken in painstaking detail. Milly's stomach turned. "The Cyclops wants to boil us," she whispered, her voice trembling. "He plans to cook us in that pot."

Louie returned to her side, tail between his legs. "I'm sorry, boy," she muttered, giving him a gentle pat. "I know it smells awful."

"Hmm..." Wolfstan stood beside her, inspecting the book. "This is a recipe for boiling chicken... Still, chicken meat isn't all that different from..." He trailed off, clearly unable to finish the thought.

"We need to tell the others," Ashley said, rubbing her temples. "Think, Ashley, think... 'I will either grill you or boil you...'" She repeated the riddle to herself before a smile broke out across her face. "It's a paradox," she said suddenly. "If we answer correctly, he'll grill us... but he wants to boil us. If we're wrong, he'll boil us anyway. So we need to give him the right answer. That way, he can't do anything."

Louie looked up at her, clearly confused. Milly wasn't much clearer. "Er..." she said. "Could you explain that again?"

"It'll make sense in a minute," Ashley assured her. "Let's get back to the others. The Cyclops might be wondering where we've gone."

"You're right," Faramund said, nodding. "Great thinking, Ashley. Let's go."

They did their best to remain inconspicuous as they made their way back to the bridge, where Catalina, Mirabel, Harry, Lucy, Fran, and Charlie were still distracting the Cyclops. Lucy had taken to playing a game of 20 Questions with him, which, Milly thought, was a smart move. At least now the Cyclops was asking questions.

The Cyclops scratched his head, frowning deeply. "Um..." he said, staring at Lucy. "Does it walk on four legs?"

"Nope!" Lucy replied, her smile bright. "Come on, Cyclops. You're running out of questions."

"We've figured out the answer to the Cyclops's riddle," Faramund said, addressing Catalina. He shuffled his feet, clearly a bit anxious. "He has a cooking pot in the centre of his cave, along with some sort of barbaric cookbook. We believe he intends to boil us, and Ashley has deduced that his riddle is actually a paradox.”

Catalina placed her hand on his shoulder. “Fantastic work, Faramund,” she praised. Turning to Ashley, who appeared somewhat embarrassed by the attention, she added, “You too, Ashley. That kind of thinking is what makes a great warrior, even more so than brute strength and bravery.” Ashley blushed deeply, and Catalina rewarded her with a dazzling smile. “So... can you explain this paradox? ‘I will either grill you or boil you... if you’re right, I will grill you; if you’re wrong, I will boil you.’” She arched an eyebrow. “Could it be that there’s no real answer since he’s not posing a question?”

“Er... that’s not it,” Ashley stammered, quickly clarifying the paradox for Catalina and the others. “Keep in mind that I’m not entirely certain I’m correct,” she said. “But it’s clear the Cyclops is expecting some sort of answer. If we provide him with the right answer, which is likely that he wants to boil us, we’ll be ‘right’ according to his riddle,”

“In which case he’ll grill us,” Lucy interjected, her expression downcast. “Nice going, Ashley.”

“No,” Ashley retorted, rolling her eyes. “If we’re right, he’ll grill us, and if we’re wrong, he’ll boil us. But the correct answer is that he intends to boil us... therefore, he won’t grill us, or do anything at all for that matter, unless he never intended to keep his word." She glanced at Mirabel. "Um… how trustworthy are Cyclopes generally?"

Mirabel shrugged. "This is only our second encounter with one," she replied. "The first was much smaller, and we ended up slaying it. I think it's safe to say that most beasts in these parts enjoy riddles, though. Let's take a chance."

Wolfstan nodded in agreement. "If he doesn't intend to keep his word, we'll do our best to slay him," he said. "I've been itching for a fight, anyway."

Everyone seemed to concur, so Catalina stepped forward and knelt before the great Cyclops. "Guardian of the bridge," she said, "we're ready to answer your riddle."

The Cyclops grinned, baring his sharp teeth. "Excellent," he said. "What is your answer, human?"

"You're going to boil us," Catalina stated confidently. "However, you've presented us with a paradox because if we're right, you'll grill us. Since you promised to boil us if we're right, though, you won't be able to do anything at all, meaning you'll have no choice but to allow us to cross the bridge."

The Cyclops pondered for a moment before sighing. "I was really looking forward to a good meal," he admitted, looking somewhat sheepish.

"Boiled knight is one of my favourite dishes... it tastes just like chicken!"

"I could really go for some chicken right now," Harry whispered to Milly. She smirked and rolled her eyes but silently agreed.

"Will you allow us to cross?" Catalina asked the giant, one-eyed beast. "Or will you give us no choice but to blind you?"

The Cyclops was quick to respond this time. "You've done well in answering my riddle," he said begrudgingly. "It appears that you and your companions are worthy enough to cross my bridge." He stepped aside, revealing the grand wooden bridge and the winding path that snaked through the mountains ahead. "May the gods and goddesses watch over you as you continue your travels."

"Well, that's nice, isn't it?" Lucy remarked as they walked across the bridge. "Maybe that Cyclops isn't such a bad chap after all."

"He was going to eat us," Milly laughed lightly, holding hands with Fran and Charlie, who kept glancing back at the Cyclops nervously.

"It's a good thing Ashley is so clever," Lucy replied. "I'd also like to take some credit for being good at 20 Questions. Just saying."

"Yeah, yeah," Ashley said, her cheeks flushing again. "You probably didn't even have a real answer to the Cyclops's questions."

Lucy chuckled. "You know me too well."

Once everyone was safely across the bridge, the group rejoiced and began their trek towards the mountains in the distance. Although Milly was relieved to have finished the ordeal with the Cyclops, she felt fatigued. Her feet ached from the long walk, and she wondered when Catalina would allow them to take a break. She could tell her brother and sister felt the same way.

"Milly," Fran said, as if on cue, "my feet hurt."

Mirabel must have overheard, for a moment later, she called out to Catalina, "Oi, Catalina! It's time to take a break, don't you think? We've been travelling all day, and the children are undoubtedly tired and hungry."

Catalina glanced back at Milly and the others. At first, Milly thought she might reprimand Mirabel, but then she smiled. "Very well," she said. "I did promise we would take a break, didn't I? We'll set up camp and get some rest before heading to the Underworld tomorrow. After all, we should conserve our strength." She beckoned for the group to follow her into the woods. They walked for several minutes until, at last, they arrived at a clearing. "This will do nicely," Catalina declared, setting down her travel bag. "Is there any more meat left, Mirabel?"

6

THE PORTAL

The next morning, after enjoying a calming breakfast of chamomile tea and fresh fruit, the group set off once more on the winding path that led to the entrance of the Underworld. Milly felt a knot forming in her stomach. What would the Underworld be like? What kinds of dangers lurked there? And how, exactly, were they going to retrieve the agate from Nyx? After their encounter with the Cyclops, she was starting to realise that in this world, cleverness and quick thinking were essential for survival. You had to trust very few people, and even less in the way of what you thought you knew. In that respect, it wasn't so different from the world she was used to, apart from the monsters and mythical creatures that seemed to be everywhere.

She glanced at Catalina, who was leading them with determination. *We still don't have weapons of our own*, Milly thought. Deciding to voice her concern, she spoke up, "Hey, Catalina? Do you think my friends and I will be able to find weapons before we get to the Underworld?"

"Certainly," Catalina replied confidently, without breaking her stride. "I know exactly where to look. On the outskirts of the Underworld, there's a place, a graveyard of sorts. It's there we'll find weapons for you and your friends."

"Can I have one, too?" Charlie piped up. "Maybe a dagger or a bow and arrows?"

"You're far too small to wield a proper bow," Wolfstan replied, trying to stifle a laugh. "If you want to help, kid, just stay out of the way. The Underworld is no place for a child, and certainly not a place to be messing around."

"We're not messing around," Fran retorted, glaring at Wolfstan. Milly admired her for standing up for her younger brother. "We might have special powers, you know. More than you have."

"Might," Wolfstan repeated, mimicking her voice. "That's helpful, isn't it?"

"There's no need to be cruel, Wolfstan," Mirabel chided, her tone soft but firm. "Charlie and Fran just want to help." She turned back to Milly's younger siblings. "Right?"

Charlie nodded firmly. "Mmhmm." He looked at Wolfstan with quiet intensity. Milly was surprised by the fire in his eyes. "I don't mean any disrespect, mister," he said, his voice steady, "but don't underestimate us because we're kids. We're a lot more capable than you think."

Wolfstan raised an eyebrow, taken aback. "Hmm..." he grunted. "Very well. Perhaps we can find some small weapons for you. But you'd better be smart about it. I don't want you running headlong into battle without thinking it through first."

The road ahead seemed endless, the sun already beating down on them as the hours ticked by. Milly began to wonder if they'd ever reach the Underworld. Finally, as if in response to her doubts, an enormous archway loomed ahead, carved from black marble, covered in twisting vines and gnarled tree branches. In the, centre of the arch, a swirling black and purple void pulsed with a low, buzzing hum, like a swarm of cicadas in a heatwave.

But what truly took Milly by surprise was what stood guarding the archway: a three-headed dog, easily twenty times the size of Louie; two women whose hair seemed made entirely of slithering snakes; and a tall, dark-robed woman, who was murmuring what sounded like incantations.

"Look at that dog," Ashley whispered, her voice barely audible. "It's huge!" Louie whimpered, tail between his legs. "Aww... it's alright, boy. We'll protect you."

"Forget about the dog," Faramund said, his voice low but firm. "Cerberus is just a guard dog. He takes orders from the gorgons. We'll need to convince them to let us into the Underworld. As long as we do that, he probably won't eat us."

"Cerberus?" Milly asked. "Is that the dog's name? Wait..." Her stomach twisted as she studied the monstrous creature again. "Is that one dog, or is it three?" Louie rushed to her side, leaping into her arms. She held him tightly, though his bulk was becoming heavy. "It's alright, boy. Gosh, he's really scared, isn't he?"

Fran shuddered. "I don't blame him," she said. "I don't like the look of those women either. Are those... snakes in their hair?"

"Those are the gorgons," Mirabel answered grimly. "Whatever you do, do *not* make eye contact with them. I mean it, not even for a second. They're said to have a deadly gaze."

Harry, looking apprehensive, asked, "How are we supposed to avoid making eye contact? We'll need to speak to them to enter the Underworld, won't we?"

"We've thought about that," Catalina replied, patting her travel bag with an air of calm authority.

"I brought along blindfolds for everyone… even Louie."

"So we'll be blind when we face them?" Milly asked, scratching Louie behind his ear. "Isn't that risky?"

Catalina nodded. "Unfortunately, we don't have much choice. But when it comes to dealing with the gorgons, I'll take the lead. Don't worry. We'll manage. The first one we need to speak to is that woman guarding the Underworld, Cerberus, and the gorgons. If I'm right, that's Agatha, the sister of Agnes."

"Right," Mirabel said, her posture relaxing slightly. "So all we need to do is tell her Agnes sent us, right?"

"In theory," Catalina said with a wry smile. "Agnes seemed confident Agatha would let us through. Though…" She glanced around warily. "We probably shouldn't mention our real reason for being here. Nyx isn't exactly worshipped in the Underworld, but she is feared. Even Zeus is afraid of her. That's what Agnes told me, anyway."

Milly felt her heart tighten. Nyx is so powerful that even Zeus fears her, she thought to herself. She took a deep breath, attempting to calm herself down. So, then… even those who are against Nyx would be too afraid of the consequences that came with allowing mere mortals to steal from her. She opened her mouth to say something, but nothing came out. Would they be able to steal from such a powerful goddess? Would Fran, Charlie, and Louie be okay? Louie was still cowering in her arms, and Fran looked a bit pale after listening to Catalina and Mirabel's conversation. "Hey," Milly said, her voice softer. "Are you alright?"

Fran nodded slowly. "Yeah, I just... I'm not sure how we're going to do this. And I'm worried about Charlie," she added, gesturing to her younger brother, who had become fixated on the massive dog. "He's so little."

"We have to believe in him," Milly replied, though her stomach was in knots. *We have to trust him.* "Um... Catalina, about that graveyard with weapons?" Milly asked, trying to shift her focus.

"Right," Catalina replied briskly. "Follow me." She led them off the path and deeper into the forest.

The branches above twisted into grotesque shapes, casting eerie shadows that danced across the forest floor. A cold wind stirred the leaves, sending shivers through Milly's spine. After what felt like an age of weaving through dense undergrowth, they arrived at a clearing bathed in an eerie light. Milly's breath caught in her throat. The so-called "graveyard" was a vast expanse of scattered bones, broken armour, and rusted weapons strewn haphazardly across the forest floor. It was as if , an entire battalion had been devoured by some monstrous beast, its remains discarded carelessly. Milly's heart pounded with a mix of fear and fascination. "This isn't a graveyard, is it, Catalina?" she whispered hoarsely. "This... this looks like a slaughter."

Catalina nodded solemnly. "Yes, I wasn't sure how to phrase it earlier. This is the site of a battle that took place many decades ago. The soldiers' bones were likely scavenged by vultures and other animals after they died." She gave a small, reassuring smile. "It's nothing to be afraid of. It's just nature in action. Now, let's look for some weapons."

Milly swallowed hard but forced herself to focus. Catalina was right. It was just nature. She had to remind herself why they were here. With a deep breath, she nodded. Harry stepped closer, taking her hand in his. "It'll be alright," he said softly. "No one's here, and some of these weapons should still be usable."

She nodded, and they began to explore the boneyard, taking special care not to step on any skeletons. Milly turned to Fran and Charlie, who were cautiously picking through the discarded gear. "You two should take those shields," she suggested. "At least that way, you'll have something to defend yourselves with."

"Okay!" Fran replied, her eyes lighting up as she hefted one of the battered shields. "It's not even that heavy!"

"But I want a real weapon!" Charlie grumbled, clearly unimpressed. "Not a stupid shield!"

Milly was in the midst of rolling her eyes when something glinted in the sunlight, a sliver of metal buried within a particularly large pile of bones. Curiosity piqued, she approached the pile, carefully brushed aside the debris, and unearthed a gleaming sword. Despite several cracks in the blade, it remained sharp, and the hilt fit comfortably in her hand. "I think I've found my weapon," she declared.

"No way," Harry exclaimed, rushing over for a closer look at Milly's sword. He had been examining a well-crafted bow several paces away, its previous owner still gripping it tightly with skeletal fingers. "That's a fantastic find, Milly." He almost looked envious. "But do you know how to use it?"

"Of course," Milly replied, playfully pointing the sword at him and swinging it slowly through the air. "I'll bet I can learn, anyway." She felt undeniably cool; just holding the sword made her heart flutter, as if it were meant for her.

"Cool sword, Milly," Ashley chimed in, brandishing a spiked mace and a rusty shield. "Have you found anything, Harry?"

"I want to use that bow over there," he said, gesturing towards the bow he had just been examining. "But that skeleton has a death grip on it... no pun intended."

"Ha!" Lucy laughed, approaching them with what appeared to be a rapier in her hand. "What's wrong, Harry? Are you afraid of a little skelly?" She smiled and pointed the rapier at him. "I always wanted to join the fencing club at school, but I never had the time. Now's my chance to use a real rapier. Isn't it cool?"

Harry grimaced. "You lot need to stop pointing sharp objects at me," he said, backing away slowly. "And no, I'm not afraid of a skeleton, Lucy. I just... feel strange prying this person's weapon from their cold, bony hands."

"I feel weird about the fact that we'll probably be giving whoever gets in our way tetanus," Ashley remarked, examining the rusty spikes on the mace she had picked up. "Uh... you all have had your tetanus shots, right?"

"Of course," Lucy replied. "You worry too much, Ash."

Milly decided to assist Harry in prying the bow from the skeleton's fingers. They approached it together, it was situated in a particularly dense area of the boneyard, forcing them to step on scattered bones, many of which crumbled to dust beneath their feet. The skeleton almost seemed to be watching them with its hollow eye sockets. Milly understood Harry's apprehension; something about it made her feel uneasy. "It's just a skeleton," she said, perhaps more to herself than to Harry. "All we have to do is unfurl its fingers and take the bow."

As Harry crouched beside the skeleton, he shivered. "It's not going to come to life, is it?" he asked, his voice barely above a whisper.

"This isn't *Pirates of the Caribbean*," Milly scoffed. "Like I said... it's just a skeleton, Harry. It's not going to do anything."

With bated breath, Harry reached out, his fingers trembling as he grasped the bow nestled in the skeleton's hand. Milly felt her heart pounding in her chest as they worked together to carefully pry the ancient weapon from its grasp. For a moment, nothing happened. The forest seemed to hold its breath, just as they did. Then, with a faint, sickening creak, the skeleton began to stir.

Milly's eyes widened in horror as the creature's bones twitched and rattled. Its empty eye sockets fixated on them, and Milly, momentarily forgetting that she was wielding a large sword, panicked. "Harry, run!" she cried, but it was too late. With a sudden lurch, the skeleton sprang to life. Its bony fingers closed around Harry's wrist, and he screamed in terror as the creature's jaws snapped shut mere inches from his face.

Milly's scream echoed through the clearing, shattering the silence like glass. The sound seemed to trigger something, as several other skeletons scattered throughout the boneyard began to stir, their bones clattering together. The commotion drew the attention of the others, who rushed over with their weapons drawn. Catalina hurled one of her throwing knives at the skeleton gripping Harry's wrist, but, to her dismay, it bounced harmlessly off its thick skull.

Mirabel and Faramund began to fend off the other skeletons, which were slowly but surely making their way towards them. Wolfstan took out skeletons left and right, notching arrow after arrow on his bow with surprising speed. Meanwhile, Ashley swung her mace with all her might. Although her swings were somewhat haphazard, she had chosen her weapon wisely, the spiked mace crashed through several skeletons, reducing their bones to dust on the ground. Throughout the chaos, Louie darted about, barking furiously as he leapt at the skeletons, his teeth bared.

Lucy, her face pale but resolute, brandished her rapier and stood protectively in front of Fran and Charlie, who held their ground despite being shaken by the sudden onslaught. They raised their shields, and Fran, who had a knack for these kinds of things, shouted at Milly, "Milly! Your sword!"

Without hesitation, Milly swung her sword at the skeleton that wouldn't release Harry, and, to her astonishment, it crumpled into a pile of bones at her feet. One by one, the skeletons fell to the ground, seemingly rejoining the realm of the dead just as quickly as they had come to life. Milly could hardly believe what she had just accomplished. The sword almost appeared to glow in her hands. She thought she must have imagined it, attributing it to the sunlight, but still, there was something peculiar about that sword. "I... can't believe that just happened. Did I really do that? Maybe my powers flowed through the sword," Milly said, helping Harry to his feet. "Is everyone okay?"

"I'm fine," Harry replied, brushing off his tunic and examining his newly acquired bow. "How about the little ones?"

"We're all right!" Charlie exclaimed. "We may need to explore your abilities a little later, but that was so cool!"

"Not exactly the word I'd use," Wolfstan said, kicking aside a pile of bones.

"Hey, Wolfstan," Harry said. "Do you think I could borrow some of your arrows?"

Wolfstan looked slightly annoyed but smiled nonetheless. "I suppose," he said. "I'll even let you have some of my sleep arrows. Just be careful with them, okay? If you accidentally jab yourself, you'll fall asleep for hours, and you don't look especially easy to carry."

After everyone had selected their weapons of choice, the group made their way towards the entrance to the Underworld. Along the way, Catalina and Mirabel shared what they knew about Nyx and the Underworld in general. "Keep in mind that this will be a new experience for us, too," Mirabel cautioned. "And finding Nyx isn't going to be easy. She resides in the deepest part of the Underworld."

"How dangerous is Nyx?" Milly asked. "And how are we going to steal her agate? Does she keep it locked up in a chest, or wear it around her neck, or..." she trailed off. The more she pondered it, the more nauseous she felt. "I feel like I'm going to throw up," she admitted.

"Uh... please don't do that," Harry said, looking a bit anxious. "We've got this, Milly. Things always work out in the end, don't they?"

"Harry's right," Ashley said, linking her elbow with Milly's. "Plus, you've got an awesome new sword. And potential powers."

"And your friends," Mirabel added. "With your friends by your side, you can achieve anything you set your mind to."

"Okay," Milly said, feeling somewhat reassured. "That's true. Let's just take it one step at a time."

"That's the spirit," Catalina encouraged. "Anyway, Nyx has a weakness. All we need to do is exploit it."

"What's her weakness?" Harry inquired.

Catalina smiled. "While you lot were searching for new clothes outside Agnes's house, she shared a bit about Nyx's family. Nyx has many children, including Nemesis... remember her?"

Milly recalled the goddess they had encountered the last time they entered Athena's Shawl, Nemesis, the goddess of revenge and retribution. Although Catalina, Mirabel, Faramund, and Wolfstan had slain her, she had returned to life and ultimately saved them from the evil priest, Deimos Asgard. If it hadn't been for Nemesis, they likely would have succumbed to Deimos Asgard. Milly's mother would probably still be in his clutches had Nemesis not swooped in like a superhero to save the day. "I remember," Milly said, her voice thick with emotion.

"Nyx is also the mother of Charon, who helps the deceased cross the River Styx, so we'll encounter him," Catalina continued. "Her other children include

Hypnos, the god of sleep, Eris, the goddess of strife and discord, and Momus, the god of scorn and ridicule."

"But what's her weakness?" Harry pressed again. "We need to know her weakness if we're going to defeat her."

"We won't be able to defeat Nyx," Mirabel interjected. "It's impossible. The plan is to sneak into the deepest part of the Underworld, take Nyx's agate, and then sneak back out. There's no need to fight Nyx, which, by the way, is a battle we would surely lose, unless absolutely necessary."

"Okay..." Harry looked slightly miffed. "But, "

"I wasn't finished," Catalina said, glaring at him. "Every family has a black sheep, right? Nyx's family is no different. Besides the gods and goddesses I've already mentioned, she has another child, a son who, despite his divinity, was tricked by the mere mortal, Sisyphus."

"Sisyphus..." Ashley said, scrunching her eyebrows. "I've read about him. He was doomed to push a boulder up a mountain, only for it to roll back down every time he almost reached the top, right?"

"That's right," Catalina confirmed. "Nyx's son, Thanatos, was tasked with taking Sisyphus to the Underworld. Sisyphus outwitted him and escaped death, at least for a time. Things didn't end well for Sisyphus, but that's somewhat irrelevant." She shook her head, as if trying to keep her thoughts from wandering. "Nyx was embarrassed by her son's failure, and they've supposedly been on bad terms ever since. Thanatos is Nyx's weakness, if we can find him, we'll be able to locate Nyx's agate."illy swallowed hard. They had navigated through the thickest part of the forest, and although she couldn't see it yet, she could hear the sniffing and panting of the three-headed dog, as well as the undulating of the portal to the Underworld. "What is Thanatos the god of?" she asked.

Catalina smiled wryly. "Death," she replied.

Minutes later, they found themselves just a few hundred metres from the enormous archway. Catalina set her travel bag down and began rifling through it, muttering to herself and cursing under her breath. Eventually, she pulled out several strips of cloth. Right, Milly thought. We'll have to blindfold ourselves to get past the gorgons. Catalina handed her four blindfolds, one for Charlie, Fran, Louie, and herself. She helped Charlie and Fran put on their blindfolds before moving on to Louie, who looked at her as if to say, You're kidding, right? He tilted his head to the side and whined. Milly understood that he probably wasn't keen on the idea of having something covering his eyes, but she remembered what Mirabel had told them. "The gorgons have a deathly gaze." She held onto Louie's collar and tried to tie the blindfold around his head as he squirmed. "Come on, boy," she coaxed. "It'll keep you safe. You primarily rely on your sense of smell, anyway, don't you?"

Louie wasn't having it. He pawed at his blindfold, whimpering softly. "Here, let me try," Fran said, lifting her blindfold to look at Louie. She crouched down beside him and placed a gentle hand on his head. "It's okay, Louie. These blindfolds will keep us safe. You only have to wear it for a few minutes, alright? Once we get past the scary ladies with the snakes in their hair, we'll take it off you. Do you understand?"

To Milly's surprise, Louie bowed his head and stopped fussing with his blindfold. Wow, she thought. Maybe Fran really can talk to animals. "Good boy," she said to Louie. Then she turned to her sister. "Fran, I'm going to leave you in charge of him, okay? I know you'll be blindfolded, but maybe you can hold onto him and sort of feel his face with your hands to make sure he can't see."

"He's not going to remove his blindfold, Milly," Fran said, beaming as she put her blindfold back on. "He told me he understands."

"Really?" Charlie asked, stumbling slightly and grabbing onto Milly's arm for support. "No joking, Fran?"

"I wouldn't joke about this," Fran insisted. She was trying to keep her voice calm, but Milly could tell how excited she was. "I told you guys I can talk to animals."

"Uh, wow…" Milly said, admittedly feeling a twinge of jealousy. "That's… that's pretty incredible." She was happy for her sister, but she couldn't help but wonder when she would discover her own special power. Being the oldest, she had thought she would be the first to find hers, but no, it was Fran. She bent down to kiss Louie and then put on her blindfold. "Is everyone ready?" she asked. "Er… should we hold hands or something so we don't trip?"

"That would be wise," Mirabel said. Milly felt a hand on her shoulder. "Milly? Is that you?" After a few moments of grasping at nothing, they found each other's hands. The others linked up too, with Catalina leading the way. "Alright, everyone," Mirabel continued. "Slowly now…" They began to make their way towards the marble archway. At least, that was what Milly assumed, she couldn't see a thing. She could hear Louie whining again as they walked, and Fran attempting to calm him down. After tripping over a few tree roots, the group finally came to a halt.

"Who goes there?" a woman's voice called. "State your business." Milly wondered if it was Agnes's sister or one of the gorgons speaking. She didn't dare remove her blindfold to find out.

"We seek entrance into the Underworld," Catalina said. "Our business is our own."

After some back and forth, the woman instructed Catalina to remove her blindfold. "I want to look you in the eyes," she said. "The gorgons are busy feeding Cerberus, so you won't have to worry about them for now."

"First, you must promise that you don't mean to harm us," Catalina said, her voice trembling slightly. "We've been sent by Agnes, who resides in Alexandria. Are you her sister, Agatha?"

The woman was silent for a moment. "Agnes..." she said. "It's been quite some time since I heard my sister's name. Can you prove that you know Agnes?"

"Um..." Catalina stammered, seemingly at a loss for words. "I... I didn't really think about that,"

"She has a cat," Ashley interjected suddenly. "Uh... I think her name is Iris."

"Hmmm..." Despite her inability to see, Milly sensed that Agatha was smiling. "Yes. My sister loves Iris. Very well," Milly heard the woman snap her fingers. "Hey, you two," she seemed to be addressing someone else, probably the gorgons. "Make sure that Cerberus understands that these travellers are friends of my sister, Agnes. And don't look at them, okay? The last thing I'd want is for my sister's companions to, uh... perish." So, she was trying to trick us into looking at the gorgons, Milly thought, her stomach churning slightly. Good thing Catalina brought these blindfolds along. "Alright. It's safe to take your blindfolds off now," Agatha said. "Sorry about before... I'm just doing my job, you know?"

One by one, they removed their blindfolds. Milly squinted against the sunlight and then took in the scene for the first time up close. The three-headed dog, Cerberus, was even larger than he appeared, and the gorgons, who had their backs turned out of respect for Agatha's orders, didn't just have snakes in their hair. No... their hair was made of live, wriggling snakes. Fran gasped at the sight and covered her eyes with her hands. Harry, Charlie, and Lucy were speechless, while Ashley, to Milly's surprise, was practically bouncing up and down in excitement. "Just look at that dog," she exclaimed for the second time. "Can... can I pet him?"

Agatha, who resembled a younger version of Agnes, arched an eyebrow. Milly, however, was too busy staring at the swirling purple portal contained within the enormous marble archway. "This is... something else," she said, taking a few steps forward.

"I know, right?" Harry said, his voice cracking slightly. "I've never seen anything like it."

"Don't get too close," Agatha warned. "I haven't let you in just yet, have I?" She turned back to face Catalina, who was clearly trying to remain calm. "State your business," she said. "You are friends of Agnes, so I know I can trust you. However," her eyes seemed to bore into Catalina's, but Catalina didn't flinch. "I must know what business you have in the Underworld if I'm going to let you in."

"We have a message for Thanatos," Catalina said without hesitation. "However, this message is only for Thanatos's ears, so we can't disclose it to you."

Agatha narrowed her eyes. "Is this a message from my sister?" she asked. "What could she possibly have to say to the god of death?"

"We can't tell you," Catalina reiterated. "But... Agnes is quite old, isn't she? And Thanatos is the god of peaceful death..."

Milly couldn't believe it. Was Catalina trying to imply that Agnes wanted to die? She assumed that Catalina was merely doing what she had to, but it was quite an outrageous lie. How was Agatha supposed to take this news, exactly? Although Agatha and Agnes were estranged, they loved each other. Nobody wants to hear that their sister wishes for death, right?

Agatha closed her eyes and nodded. "Ah, yes," she said, a sad smile spreading across her lips. "I already knew that my sister's time was near. She's 197 years old, after all..." She opened her eyes again and placed her hand on Catalina's shoulder. "Please deliver your message to Thanatos and ensure that my sister rests in peace. You'll be doing me a huge favour." She snapped her fingers at the gorgons again, and Cerberus let out a tremendous bark. Louie barked back at him, still a little nervous about being in the presence of a giant dog with multiple heads. His anxiety seemed to be melting into curiosity, which made Milly happy. "Cerberus..." Agatha said. "Step aside so that our guests can enter the Underworld." Cerberus whined as if he didn't quite trust Catalina and the others. "Cerberus..." the old woman spoke to him in the same tone Milly's mother sometimes used when Louie was in trouble.

The enormous dog huffed and moved aside, allowing the group to pass. The gorgons followed suit, speaking to him in gentle voices and petting his sleek, black fur. At this point, Louie could no longer contain himself. Before Milly could react, he dashed right up to Cerberus, seemingly deciding that he was a friend. He wagged his tail and assumed a playful stance, with his front feet forward and his tail held high. Louie was about the size of Cerberus's paw, and Milly couldn't help but chuckle at the thought of them playing together. Cerberus looked down at Louie with curiosity, tilting one of his heads to the side, while the middle head lolled its giant tongue out.

"Come on, Louie," Milly called, clapping her hands to beckon him back. "Maybe you can play later."

Louie barked at Cerberus one last time before obediently running back to Milly and the others. Before stepping into the portal, she held hands with Fran and Charlie. "Promise me you won't run off on your own," she said, eyeing Charlie in particular. "The Underworld is a dangerous place. It's not somewhere to mess around."

"We won't, Milly," Charlie assured her. "We'll stay by your side. We promised Mum."

"Yeah," Fran added, gazing at the purple portal in awe. She picked up Louie and cradled him in her arms. "Everything will be alright as long as we stick together. We don't plan on wandering off."

Milly nodded, and, following closely behind Catalina and the others, she stepped through the portal, hand in hand with her brother and sister.

7

THE GOD OF DEATH

The first thing Milly noticed about the Underworld was its overwhelming darkness. However, the darkness wasn't, frightening; if anything, it was surprisingly comforting, wrapping around her like a thick, warm blanket. It was also unexpectedly cold, a stark contrast to what she had imagined. Milly had assumed that the Underworld would be blisteringly hot and filled with the sounds of people screaming in agony, but it was, in fact, rather... peaceful here. Of course, this was merely the entrance. God only knows what lies beyond the River Styx, she thought to herself, her mind racing with possibilities. She could see and hear the mythical river flowing and babbling just a short distance away, its waters glistening in the dim light. A rocky path led them to a rather ordinary-looking dock, where a long wooden boat bobbed gently in the water, its presence both inviting and foreboding.

The boat's captain was a skeletal man, no, a living skeleton, clad in a flowing red robe that contrasted sharply with his bony frame. He extended his bony hand, not uttering a word, but seemingly waiting for something before inviting them on board. Catalina, ever the leader, distributed a gold coin to each of, them, including one for Louie, and then placed her coin into the skeleton's outstretched hand, with everyone else following suit in a somewhat nervous silence.

Milly and Harry exchanged glances, a shared sense of unease passing between them. "Great," Harry whispered, his voice barely above a murmur. "More skeletons."

Catalina tentatively took the skeleton's hand and stepped onto the boat, the others following suit with a mix of trepidation and curiosity. "You must be Charon," she said, looking a little uneasy as she addressed the skeletal figure. The skeleton nodded, sending a chill down Milly's spine. "You may have heard that we've come to deliver a message to Thanatos," Catalina continued, her voice steady despite the circumstances. "Can you take us to him?"

Charon nodded again, picked up his large oars, and began to row the boat down the River Styx. Silence enveloped them for several minutes, a heavy blanket of quiet that felt almost oppressive. Perhaps they were unnerved by Charon's eerie silence, or maybe they simply didn't know what to say. The only sounds were the splashes of Charon's massive oars dipping into the water and the faint babbling of the river. Milly tried to avoid getting wet, recalling something from her history textbook about a demigod named Achilles, who had been dipped into the River Styx as an infant by his mother. His mother had been reluctant to touch the river herself, as it had the power to grant immortality to those who submerged themselves. The only part of Achilles that remained dry was his heel, which his mother had held onto while dipping him into the river. Many people learned this, and Achilles was eventually struck in the heel by an arrow, the only way he could be killed. Maybe he shouldn't have worn sandals, Milly thought, chuckling to herself, which earned her an odd look from Lucy.

"What are you laughing about?" she whispered, her voice tinged with concern. "This is no time for laughter. That skeleton is so creepy."

"Oh, nothing," Milly replied, feeling a bit foolish for her moment of levity. It was still hard for her to believe that she was here, riding in a boat down the River Styx. Dim light flickered from the torches lining the riverbank, and the air was heavy with the scent of earth and decay. A sense of unease gnawed at Milly's insides as they ventured deeper into the heart of the Underworld. As they glided downstream, the landscape began to shift around them. Milly's eyes darted nervously from side to side, searching for any sign of the mythical creatures said to inhabit this realm. For a while, she saw little, just darkness and jagged shapes here and there.

The air grew humid, and after several minutes, they entered a thick mist that made it somewhat difficult to breathe. Then, she spotted a wooden sign illuminated briefly by one of the torches. "Asphodel Meadows," it read. The mist seemed to dissipate, and Charon rowed the boat past what appeared to be a vast expanse of rolling plains and twisted trees. The landscape was eerily still, with no signs of life save for the occasional flicker of movement in the shadows. It seemed to be a place of indifference, where the souls of those who had lived neither good nor bad lives wandered for eternity.

Milly shivered as they passed through the desolate landscape, the sense of emptiness weighing heavily on her soul. As Charon continued rowing, the darkness began to lift, revealing a breathtaking scene: a lush, green landscape where people and animals appeared to be living quite happily in modest homes alongside the river. She noticed another wooden sign that read "Elysium." Mirabel quickly explained that Elysium was where the souls of heroes and virtuous mortals were said to reside. Milly's breath caught in her throat as she beheld the beauty of this place. The air was filled with the scent of flowers and the chirping of birds. The rolling hills seemed to stretch on forever, and she couldn't help but feel a sense of peace wash over her. It was as if the very essence of this place had seeped into her bones. She almost felt regret that they couldn't explore Elysium, but she knew they had more pressing matters to attend to.

As they continued their journey down the River Styx, the atmosphere grew increasingly tense. The once serene waters now churned ominously beneath them, and a heavy silence settled over the group, broken only by the gentle lapping of the river against the sides of the boat. Milly's heart raced as they drifted further into the darkness. Then, she spotted it, a wooden sign just ahead, its letters etched in dark, twisted script. "Tartarus," it read. A wave of dread washed over her as she realised where they were headed. Tartarus, she assumed, was likely the darkest and most dreaded region of the Underworld, a place of eternal punishment where the souls of the wicked were condemned to suffer for all eternity. It was where Nyx and her children resided.

"Um... Milly?" Fran tugged at the sleeve of her tunic, her voice trembling. "Do you see that?" She pointed at something that made Milly's heart drop into her stomach, a massive waterfall in the distance.

They were headed straight for it. The roar of the rushing water grew louder with each passing second.

"Charon, stop!" she cried, her voice ringing out in desperation. But the skeletal boatman remained silent, his eyes fixed straight ahead as he continued to row. Frantic shouts erupted from the group as they realised the danger they were in. Lucy gripped her rapier tightly, her knuckles turning white with fear. Ashley clutched her mace with trembling hands, and Mirabel drew her sword, as if such a thing would help at a time like this. Then, with a sickening lurch, the boat plunged over the edge of the waterfall, hurtling downwards into the abyss below.

Milly screamed, gripping the sides of the boat as they plummeted down the waterfall. Louie howled along with her, and she felt a pang of sympathy for him. He probably had no idea what was happening and was terrified out of his wits. Fran was holding onto Milly's elbow, her eyes tightly shut, while Charlie's face appeared frozen in a silent scream. After what felt like hours of falling, and perhaps it was hours, the waterfall flattened out, and they found themselves, seemingly unscathed, at the bottom.

As they took in their surroundings, Milly felt a wave of stifling heat wash over her. The air was thick with the stench of sulphur and brimstone. The landscape was starkly different from that of Elysium, instead of trees, animals, and quaint cottages, it was filled with jagged rocks and seething lava. The ground cracked and fissured beneath their feet from the intense heat. In the distance, she could see shadowy figures writhing in torment, their anguished cries echoing through the air. It was a scene straight out of her worst nightmares, a place of unimaginable suffering and despair. After climbing out of the boat, still a bit disoriented from the great fall, Charon turned to them, an eerie smile spreading across his bony lips. "We're here," he said, his voice echoing ominously.

As they walked along the narrow stone trail that twisted and turned through the depths of Tartarus, Milly couldn't help but feel numb to the suffering surrounding her. Everywhere she looked, someone was being tortured. Huge, black serpents slithered through the lava, and Fran and Charlie clung to her as if their lives depended on it. She began to wonder, Is this too much? Am I in over my head here? Surely, their mother wouldn't approve of them traversing this hellscape. She tried to push the thought aside and turned to look at Harry, who was sweating profusely through his tunic. "You alright?" she whispered, intending to speak more audibly.

Harry nodded, though his expression was strained. "You?"

"Yeah," Milly replied, her brow furrowed with concern. "I'm just... really worried about the little ones and Louie. What if this is too much for them?"

"Hey, you're the ones who wanted to tag along," Wolfstan retorted, glancing back at them. "You can't really complain, can you?" His irritation was palpable, exacerbated by the sweltering heat. He certainly wasn't alone in that sentiment.

"I'm so sick of your whining, Milly," Lucy interjected sharply, her voice cutting through the tension. "You claim to be worried about Fran, Charlie, and Louie, but it's really just about whether you can handle it yourself." She wiped the sweat from her brow with the sleeve of her tunic. "Which, clearly, you can't. I knew this would happen."

"Hey... come on," Mirabel interjected, attempting to diffuse the tension. "Let's take a breather for a moment, shall we? I have some water left in my bag." Everyone eagerly seized the opportunity to sip from Mirabel's canteen. Milly made sure Louie got his share, allowing him to take a few generous laps from her modest capful. He looked up at her with his big, puppy-dog eyes, panting heavily but appearing a bit more refreshed. She wished her mum had taken him to the groomers before they left; his heavy fur coat, was a burden in this heat. But there was no way her mother could have anticipated that they would be trudging through the depths of the Underworld. She wouldn't have wanted to know that, anyway.

After drinking some water and nibbling on a piece of rather melted fruit, Milly settled down next to Ashley, who seemed lost in thought. "What's up?" Milly asked her friend, concern etched on her face. "You feeling okay?"

"Oh, um, yeah," Ashley replied, forcing a smile that didn't quite reach her eyes. "It's just hot." She glanced around at the others. Fran and Charlie sat in silence next to Mirabel, while Harry leaned his head against the rocky wall, sweat trickling through his hair. Wolfstan, Faramund, and Catalina were embroiled in a heated discussion about various topics, the oppressive heat, the arduous journey, and whether their plan to collaborate with Thanatos would even succeed, not to mention the physical limitations of the children who had 'tagged along.' Ashley sighed, her voice filled with resignation. "Things are looking pretty bleak, aren't they? I thought this was going to be a fun adventure like last time, but..." She trailed off, her expression clouded with doubt. "Ah, well. How are you

holding up, Milly?"

Milly hesitated, unsure how to respond. "I'm okay," she said, glancing from Fran to Charlie to Harry. She stole a look at Lucy, who sat against the wall next to Harry, her head cradled in her hands. "I think Lucy's mad at me," she whispered, her voice barely audible.

"Oh, don't worry about her," Ashley reassured her, her tone soothing. "You know how hot-headed she can be. Once we find Thanatos, retrieve the agate, and get the heck out of here, we'll be fine." She pursed her lips and took a deep breath. "We should keep moving," she suggested after a few moments. "Maybe not everyone has to go the whole way? Perhaps Fran and Charlie could wait for us in a safer spot in the Underworld while we retrieve Nyx's agate. They seem to have taken a shine to Mirabel, do you think she'd mind looking after them?"

"Huh," Milly mused, raising an eyebrow. It wasn't a bad idea. That said, she wasn't sure how enthusiastic Mirabel would be about babysitting Fran and Charlie. "You're onto something, Ash. If we have the little ones wait in Elysium with Mirabel, we won't have to worry about them getting hurt."

"Exactly," Ashley said, hoisting herself off the ground and offering Milly a slightly dirty hand. "Come on. Let's talk to Mirabel."

Fran and Charlie were less than pleased about having to return to Elysium with Mirabel while the others continued their journey through Tartarus. Fran wouldn't even look at Milly after she suggested it, and

Charlie protested for a good five minutes before finally relenting and taking Mirabel by the hand. Mirabel, however, appeared quite content with the arrangement. Milly suspected she was fed up with Catalina and the others and was looking forward to some quiet time in the paradise-like part of the Underworld with Fran and Charlie. "Come along, children," she said, patting Charlie on the head and giving Fran a friendly smile. "You saw how lovely Elysium is while that nice man in the boat was rowing us here, didn't you? You'll love it there."

Louie bounded over to Fran and Charlie, showering them with big kisses, which seemed to lift their spirits a little.

Milly bid a temporary farewell to her siblings, reminding them to behave. "We'll swing by Elysium once we've retrieved the agate," she said, giving Fran a serious look. "Be ready to jump in Charon's boat, okay?"

"Okay," Fran replied, appearing a bit more agreeable now, despite her disappointment. "You'll tell us all about the deepest part of the Underworld, won't you?" She placed her hands on her hips, her expression earnest. "You'd better not leave anything out, Milly. We might not be able to handle the heat and the distance we have to walk, but we deserve to hear the story and look after Louie."

Milly nodded, her heart swelling with affection for her siblings. "I'll tell you everything later. I promise, and don't lose the coins Catalina gave you, or you'll be stuck on this side." She quickly hugged her brother and sister. Louie jumped up to Fran, giving her a big kiss on the cheek before scampering off to join Catalina and Wolfstan at the front of the group, seemingly invigorated. Milly waved goodbye once more and tore herself away from her siblings and Mirabel as the group pressed onward. She found herself walking between Harry, who was still drenched in sweat, and Lucy, who hadn't uttered a word since her earlier outburst. "Hey, um..." she ventured to Lucy. "Are you okay?"

Lucy shot her an irritated glance. "Yes," she replied, though her tone suggested otherwise. "It's just hot. I hope we reach our destination soon." She craned her neck to look at Catalina, who was confidently leading them toward what appeared to be a tomb with a large boulder blocking the entrance. "Oi!" Lucy called out. "Are we almost there?"

"She's quite impatient, isn't she?" Harry remarked, gently nudging Milly with his elbow. "Sheesh. We'll get there when we get there."

"It won't be long now," Catalina assured them, glancing back. "We're about to enter... um... what I suppose you could call the residential area of

Tartarus. I saw a depiction of it in one of Agnes's books. I'm not entirely sure which tomb belongs to Thanatos, but we're on the right path."

As they ventured deeper into Tartarus, the heat seemed to intensify, wrapping around them like a suffocating blanket. Milly wiped the sweat from her brow, the beads of moisture clinging to her skin in the stifling air. She cast a worried glance at Lucy, whose frustration was evident as they trudged through the fiery landscape. The so-called residential area of Tartarus was a labyrinth of crumbling tombs and twisted pathways, the architecture ancient and foreboding. The walls were adorned with grotesque carvings and ominous symbols. Milly thought she recognized a few from her history textbook, but the meanings eluded her.

As they walked, Milly couldn't shake the unsettling feeling of being watched. She hugged herself tightly, a chill running down her spine despite the oppressive heat. Catalina continued to lead the way, her expression set in grim determination. She paused in front of a towering tomb and reached for one of the skull-shaped knockers that adorned the enormous golden door. Then, she hesitated. "Okay, so I think this is where Thanatos lives," she said. "But I'm not completely sure. This might be dangerous, so you lot should stand back," she gestured at Milly, Ashley, Lucy, and Harry. "I'm going to knock and see if he answers." She reached for the knocker again, her hand trembling slightly. "Thanatos?" She knocked three times and waited several minutes, but nothing happened. "Hello? Is anyone home?"

"What business do you have here?" a young man's voice called from behind them. Catalina jumped and spun around to face the mysterious speaker. Milly and the others followed suit, surprised to see a strikingly handsome, muscular man with long white hair and enormous black raven wings sprouting from his shoulder blades. Louie barked and growled at him for what felt like an eternity before retreating behind Milly's legs. The young man raised an eyebrow at the group. "It's not often that I receive visitors," he remarked, his tone both curious and wary. Catalina appeared taken aback, either by the young man's appearance or by the fact he had approached them so stealthily.

"Are... are you Thanatos?" Catalina stammered, clearing her throat in an attempt to gather her wits. "Uh... of course you are," she added, shrinking slightly under his scrutinising gaze. "We're from the Overworld. We've... uh... come to seek your guidance."

The young man regarded Catalina with a sceptical expression. He approached her and leaned against the door that barred the tomb's entrance, pushing his hair out of his eyes and folding his arms across his chest with a sigh. Milly couldn't help but feel a flutter of admiration. "Yes... I am Thanatos," he replied, his tone tinged with annoyance. "And you are?"

"We're adventurers," Wolfstan interjected, stepping forward, clearly noticing that Catalina was struggling to maintain her composure. "We've been sent here on an important quest, and... well... given your history with your mother, we thought you might be able to help."

Thanatos blinked, his expression shifting from cool and collected to defensive and angry in an instant. "What has this got to do with my mother?" he demanded, his voice rising slightly. "Explain yourselves at once!" Louie, seemingly regaining his courage, dashed up to Thanatos and began tugging at his robes with his teeth. Milly, horrified, leapt forward and grabbed hold of him. He squirmed in her arms for a moment before going limp like a rag doll. "What is that?" Thanatos pointed at Louie, his brow furrowing in confusion. "Is that supposed to be a dog?"

"Yes, he's a dog," Milly replied, slightly offended on Louie's behalf. Louie shifted in her arms to glare at Thanatos, his loyalty evident.

"He's not like any dog I've seen," Thanatos remarked, his tone a mix of curiosity and disdain.

"Anyway... can you please explain what sort of quest you're on? It's unusual for humans to come to the Underworld willingly." He scrutinised Milly with a piercing gaze, making her feel exposed. "It's even stranger to see children here, ."

"We're not children," Harry interjected, his voice firm. "Or, I guess we technically are... but we're more capable than you might think. Milly's even capable of using magic, ."

"Harry! Don't tell him that," Milly hissed through clenched teeth, panic rising in her chest. "I don't even know yet if I actually have powers, remember?" Thanatos let out a cold laugh that sent a shiver down Milly's spine. She exchanged worried glances with Ashley, who seemed to share her unease. Can we really trust this guy?

"Look... Thanatos," Catalina said, finally regaining her composure. "I'll get straight to the point, okay? We need something from your mother to complete our quest. Her agate, to be exact. Do you happen to know where she keeps it?"

Thanatos's expression shifted dramatically. He looked fearful, but there was something else in his eyes, excitement? No... vengeance. "Keep your voice down," he whispered, quickly opening the door to allow them into his tomb. "My mother has spies everywhere. We should discuss this inside."

The interior of Thanatos's tomb was unlike anything Milly had ever encountered. The walls were adorned with intricate carvings depicting scenes from ancient battles, tales of gods and monsters that seemed to come alive in the flickering light. A soft glow emanated from the ceiling, casting long shadows across the chamber. Thanatos led them deeper into the tomb, his footsteps echoing off the stone walls. The air was thick with the scent of decay, which made Milly want to cover her mouth and nose with the sleeve of her tunic. She noticed that Lucy and Ashley were doing just that and followed suit, hoping Thanatos wouldn't mind. It made sense that his tomb would smell of death, after all, he was the God of Death.

"Good God… it stinks in here," Harry remarked, lacking tact as always.

"You don't like it?" Thanatos asked, genuinely surprised. "I think it's rather nice. However, I don't usually get visitors. Perhaps I've grown too accustomed to the scent of my own home."

Finally, they reached a small alcove hidden behind a tapestry that depicted an ancient painting of Thanatos himself, his features striking and proud. This guy sure is full of himself, Milly thought, suppressing a smirk. Thanatos motioned for them to sit while he paced back and forth, his mind clearly racing. After a moment of tense silence, Milly cleared her throat. "So... about Nyx's agate..."

Thanatos halted in his tracks and turned to face them, his expression shifting to one of intense focus. "You want to use the agate to enter Alexander the Great's Tomb. Isn't that right?"

Milly exchanged surprised glances with the others, her heart racing at the revelation.

"How did you know?" Harry asked, his voice filled with disbelief.

Thanatos let out a bitter laugh. "Because I know my mother all too well. She's always had a fascination with that tomb, ever since Alexander's death. She's convinced there's an object of power beyond your imagination hidden within, something that could make her even more powerful than she already is if she managed to get her hands on it."

Catalina nodded, her expression serious. "And you want to help us because..."

"Because I'm tired of being treated like an embarrassment," Thanatos replied, his voice laced with resentment. "My mother has never once shown me any respect. She sees me as nothing more than a pawn in her game. But if I help you steal her agate, it will be the first step towards proving to her that I'm actually worth something."

With a somewhat sinister smile, Catalina glanced around at the others. Her eyes seemed to convey a message: See? I told you so. Milly felt a surge of excitement mixed with anxiety bubbling in her stomach. Yet, she couldn't shake the nagging feeling of guilt that loomed over her. Why does everything we do have to involve lies and deception? she pondered. Good people don't lie, do they? A part of her recognised that using Thanatos to achieve their goals felt wrong, ; after all, he seemed like a decent enough bloke. Another part understood that the situation was far more complicated. Besides, she could think of several heroes who were tricksters, Odysseus, Captain Jack Sparrow, and even Batman. We're just doing what's necessary, she reassured herself. It's all going to be okay.

"Now, keep in mind that stealing Nyx's agate will be no easy task," Thanatos continued, his tone shifting to one of seriousness. "I also don't work for free. I expect something in return."

"Okay..." Catalina replied cautiously, her brow furrowing. "So, what do you want?"

He stepped closer to Catalina, who had wiped the smile from her face, now looking at him with apprehension. He leaned in so close that their noses almost touched, and then, with that sweet, velvety voice of his, he said, "Your life."

Just then, Louie let out a series of howls that sent shivers through the assembled group, breaking the tension in the air. Milly felt her heart race as she processed the gravity of the situation. What had they gotten themselves into?

8

ESCAPE FROM THE UNDERWORLD

Catalina took a step back, her eyes wide with disbelief. The others exchanged uneasy glances, unsure of how to respond to Thanatos's demand. "My life?" Catalina repeated, her voice barely above a whisper.

Thanatos nodded solemnly. "That's right. If I'm going to risk angering my mother by helping you steal her agate, I need to ensure my own safety. And what better guarantee than the life of the one who leads this odd little group of adventurers?" Louie began to growl again, straining against Milly's hold as she tightened her grip on him.

Catalina's mind raced as she weighed her options. She understood how crucial obtaining Nyx's agate was to their quest, but she couldn't simply sacrifice her own life in exchange. Not without a fight, at least. "I can't do that," Catalina said, her voice trembling slightly. "It's not fair. I won't sacrifice my life for this."

Thanatos's expression hardened, though a hint of resignation flickered in his eyes. "Very well," he replied, his voice devoid of emotion. "But then I can't help you either. You'll have to find another way to obtain Nyx's agate."

Catalina sighed and rubbed her temples. "I honestly didn't think this would happen," she confided to the others.

"It's okay," Milly reassured her. "I don't want you to sacrifice your life, Catalina. It's not worth it." Yet Milly could sense that something was brewing in Catalina's mind, perhaps a brilliant plan? She hoped that was the case, but either way, she wasn't going to let Catalina sacrifice herself. They would have to find a different way to steal Nyx's agate. Before anyone could say anything further, Thanatos turned on his heel and began to walk away.

"Wait," Catalina called after him, her voice quivering slightly. "There has to be another way."

Thanatos paused, his back still turned to them. "There is," he said. "But it won't be easy."

Catalina exchanged a hopeful glance with the others before stepping forward to confront Thanatos once more. "Tell us what we need to do," she urged.

"We'll find a way to retrieve Nyx's agate without putting anyone's life at risk."

Thanatos turned to face them, a small smile forming at the corners of his lips. "Very well," he said, his tone lighter than before. "If you're willing to take the risk, then I'll help you. But remember, stealing Nyx's agate will be no easy task. She's a powerful goddess, and she won't take kindly to anyone trying to take what's hers." He leaned against the wall, appearing almost nonchalant. "Long ago," he began, "my mother stole something from me. She keeps it in a small bottle on the shelf that occupies the far side of the room. You won't have an easy time finding it, she keeps it among all her potion bottles, but it has a distinct appearance. I've been too afraid to try and steal it myself..." he trailed off.

"What is it?" Milly asked. "What does it look like?"

Thanatos gave her a solemn look. "My joy," he replied. "That witch stole my ability to be happy." His mouth formed a thin line, and then he closed his eyes, taking a deep breath. "The bottle will be filled with a golden liquid. It should stand out among the purple and black potion bottles, but it's tiny, so you might have a hard time finding it regardless. I never really had that much joy to begin with." He ran a hand through his hair and sighed. "Nevertheless, I'd like it back. If you manage to steal my joy back from Nyx," he turned to face Catalina, "I won't take your life."

"She stole your joy?" Ashley interjected. "That's terrible."

"Yes," Thanatos replied. "That's just how my mother is."

"We'll get it back for you," Catalina assured him. "Along with Nyx's agate. It'll be easy." She shared a glance with Wolfstan, who appeared somewhat anxious. "Don't worry," she said, though Milly wondered if she was trying to reassure herself more than Wolfstan, after all, her life was at stake. "We can do this. We just need to devise a plan."

"That's right," Milly chimed in, doing her best to encourage Catalina and the others. "We've been through the wringer already. This'll be nothing!"

Thanatos nodded, a flicker of gratitude crossing his features. "Thank you," he said quietly. "I appreciate your willingness to help."

Catalina took charge as usual. "Alright," she said. "We'll wait until nightfall, then sneak into Nyx's bedroom while she's sleeping. Do you happen to know where she keeps her agate, Thanatos?"

Thanatos nodded. "She keeps it in a music box underneath her bed," he informed them. "So, just take the music box and don't open it. Obviously."

"Right," Catalina grinned. "Okay, so Wolfstan and Ashley will steal the music box from underneath Nyx's bed. I believe you two are the stealthiest among us, so you shouldn't have any trouble." She turned to Milly, Harry, and Lucy. "Can I trust you three to find the bottle Thanatos mentioned? Milly, you've got a keen eye, haven't you?"

Milly gulped. "Keen enough," she replied, though Louie squirmed in her arms, whining a bit.

"What should Louie do?"

"Uh... Louie probably shouldn't go anywhere near Nyx's bedroom," Faramund suggested. "He's much too loud."

"Oh," Milly said, looking a little disappointed. "He knows how to be quiet, though. Don't you, Louie?" Louie barked loudly, looking excited, which didn't exactly instill Milly with confidence. "Alright..." she said. "Well, maybe someone can keep an eye on Louie while we're sneaking around in Nyx's bedroom. It's probably better for a smaller group to carry out this mission, anyway."

Catalina nodded in agreement. "I believe that would be for the best," she said. "Faramund will watch Louie and make sure that he keeps quiet. You can handle that, right Faramund?"

Faramund looked rather offended. "You're putting me on Louie duty?" He frowned. "Fine... but he better not run off."

Milly thought she saw the shadow of a smile on Catalina's lips. "Okay, then," Catalina said, clasping her hands together. "Thanatos and I will take out the guards, because I assume there'll be guards, right?" She looked at Thanatos, who gave a minuscule nod. "Of course," she sighed. "Well... we won't know whether we'll succeed until we try."

When night finally fell, Thanatos began to lead the group towards Nyx's tomb. Faramund had decided to take Louie to Elysium, and Milly agreed. Louie had looked back at Milly as he was led away, unsure of the plan and concerned for everyone's safety. "Come on, boy, they will be safe," Faramund said as he trudged off, holding the two gold coins that Catalina had given him.

He would be safest there, after all, and he would probably be happy to see Fran and Charlie. The journey through Tartarus was as treacherous as ever, the air was hot even at night, and the voices of lost souls echoed against the walls. Milly and the others forged ahead, their steps sure and steady. As they approached the entrance to Nyx's tomb, Milly's heart pounded with anticipation. She could see the two skeleton guards standing watch, their empty eye sockets glaring menacingly.

Without hesitation, Catalina reached for her throwing knives, her movements swift and precise. With a flick of her wrist, she sent one of the knives flying towards the nearest guard, striking it square in the chest and sending it crumbling to the ground. Meanwhile, Thanatos moved with surprising speed, his powerful arms wrapping around the second guard's neck in a vice-like grip. With a muffled grunt, the guard slumped to the ground, unconscious.

With the guards dealt with, Catalina signalled for the others to follow her as they slipped through the entrance to Nyx's bedroom. As Milly's eyes adjusted to the darkness, she couldn't help but notice that the room was more beautiful and elegant than she had ever imagined. Purple and gold curtains adorned the windows, while massive paintings framed in silver lined the walls. In the centre of the room, Nyx lay sleeping on a plush velvet bed, her long black hair cascading around her like a veil. She was dressed in a flowing gown of midnight purple, her features serene in slumber.

Catalina gestured for Ashley and Wolfstan to begin the task of stealing the music box. She kept watch at the door alongside an extremely nervous-looking Thanatos, while Milly, Harry, and Lucy fanned out to search for the golden liquid among Nyx's potion bottles, Thanatos's bottled joy. Nyx's shelf, filled with potions, was no trifling matter; it occupied the entire back wall of her bedroom, and the potion bottles, brimming with sickening black and purple liquids, emitted a strange aroma. Milly covered her nose with her tunic sleeve and began to search the shelf alongside Harry and Lucy. She tried to be as quiet as possible, but it was challenging to sift through the various potion bottles without making noise.

Meanwhile, Ashley and Wolfstan crept towards Nyx's bed. Ashley lay on her stomach and cautiously reached a hand beneath the bed while Wolfstan kept a watchful eye on the sleeping goddess. After several minutes, Milly heard Harry gasp. He was holding a medium-sized bottle containing a dark red potion. It wasn't Thanatos's joy, but whatever it was, it clearly piqued his interest. She tiptoed over to where Harry stood, and he showed her the bottle. Its label, written in loopy calligraphy, read: "Lust #9." Milly rolled her eyes and silently motioned for Harry to put the bottle back. Then she spotted it. Hidden behind several large bottles of purple gunk was a tiny bottle filled with glowing golden liquid. "Look," she whispered, nudging Harry with her elbow. "That has to be it." She caught Lucy's attention and beckoned her to join them. Lucy saw the bottle and pumped her fist into the air, her mood evidently lifted.

Suddenly, they heard a noise from the other side of the room, Ashley retrieving the music box from beneath Nyx's bed, accompanied by Wolfstan's muttered curses. Milly's heart skipped a beat; they weren't as stealthy as they had hoped. Thanatos and Catalina stood nervously by the door, their eyes darting back and forth as they kept watch for any sign of danger. As the minutes passed, however, it became clear that Nyx was a heavy sleeper. Lucy quickly snatched the little golden bottle, she was, after all, the most agile among them, and made her way toward Catalina and Thanatos, with Milly and Harry following closely behind. Wolfstan and Ashley joined them moments later, the music box safely tucked under Ashley's arm.

They had succeeded in their mission. With a triumphant smile, Lucy held up the small bottle containing Thanatos's joy, the golden liquid shimmering slightly. Thanatos let out a sigh of relief, his eyes shining with gratitude.

"We did it," Catalina whispered. "We did it! Great job, everyone!" Just then, they heard Nyx stirring in her bed. Everyone held their breath, praying that she wouldn't wake up, but it was in vain. Her eyes shot open, and Thanatos grabbed Lucy's wrist, desperate to keep his bottle of joy away from his devious mother.

"We have to go now!" Thanatos hissed, prising the bottle from Lucy's fingers. "Run!"

Panic surged through the group as they scrambled to make their escape. Thanatos led the way, his eyes darting frantically for any sign of danger. With Nyx stirring behind them, they knew they had to move quickly. Catalina grasped Milly's hand, pulling her along as they raced through Tartarus. "We must rely on Charon to take us to Elysium," she said. "We'll be safe there, and we can meet up with the others."

Milly could feel her heart pounding in her chest. She could hardly comprehend what was happening around her, all she could do was focus on moving forward. Her lungs burned as she made her way towards Charon's boat. Harry was close behind her, and Ashley brought up the rear, the music box still clutched tightly in her arms.

As they approached the shores of the River Styx, Charon's boat emerged from the swirling mist, a dark silhouette against the fog. Milly's heart leapt with hope at the sight of their means of escape. Catalina led the group towards the boat, her steps quick and determined. She exchanged a hurried glance with Charon and handed a small number of coins into his outstretched hand. He nodded in understanding, and without a word, he began to push the boat into the murky waters of the river. Milly climbed aboard, her hands trembling with adrenaline as she helped Harry and Ashley onto the boat. She glanced back towards the entrance to Nyx's tomb, half-expecting to see the goddess herself pursuing them, but there was no sign of Nyx, only the echoing cries of her anger fading into the distance. With a shudder of relief, Milly turned her attention back to the task at hand. Then she realised something. "Hey," she said. "Where's Thanatos?"

Catalina craned her neck around and pointed at the figure in the distance, Thanatos in all his glory. "I don't think he can come with us," she said. "Many of the gods that reside in the Underworld cannot leave. He may very well be one of them." She waved at him as if to say thank you. "I'm glad we helped him get his joy back."

As Charon rowed the boat along the River Styx, the group huddled together, their hearts still racing from their narrow escape. They sailed towards the safety of Elysium, and Milly couldn't help but feel a surge of relief. Their quest was far from over, but they had faced their greatest challenge yet. All they had to do now was find Alexander's tomb. First, though, they had to locate Fran, Charlie, Louie, and the others in Elysium. She hoped they would be waiting near the shore, that way, they'd be able to jump onto Charon's boat. She looked at Charon and felt a strong sense of gratitude for him. She knew he was just doing his job, but they'd have to tip him extra.

9

THE TOMB OF ALEXANDER

Fran, Charlie, and Louie were overjoyed by their time in Elysium, so much so that Charlie threw a tantrum when Milly announced it was time to leave. "I would have happily stayed there for the rest of my life," he grumbled, sulking as Charon rowed the boat down a gentler stretch of the River Styx. "Mum would have loved it in Elysium."

"You'll have to tell her all about it later, or maybe not; she'll probably freak out and ground us," Milly replied. She couldn't help but glance behind them frequently. Was Nyx still following them? Could she still follow them? And what would happen to Thanatos? "We obviously couldn't leave you two there, Charlie. I promised Mum I'd bring you back home." Louie, however, had been delighted to see Milly and had run around in circles with excitement. He jumped into her arms, burying his head in Milly's lap and letting out a soft whine. "Aw, not you too, Louie! Did you enjoy it there as well?" she asked, handing him a Louie chewie, which he accepted with obvious delight. "One minute you lot are complaining about leaving Tartarus to come to Elysium, and now you don't want to leave Elysium? Give me a break."

Mirabel and Faramund chuckled from the back of the boat. "Well, it was rather lovely," Mirabel said. "It's impossible to describe. You just feel... at peace, there. Like nothing bad could happen."

"I never knew there could be a place like that in the Underworld," Ashley said. "A place like Heaven."

"There didn't used to be," Catalina explained. "Hades created it for his one great love, Persephone."

"Hmm..." Ashley frowned. "I read that Hades kidnapped Persephone." Milly tried to recall what she was talking about and realised Ashley was right. Mr. Hayes had given a lecture on the myth of Persephone and her relationship with Hades. There was certainly more to the Underworld than she'd ever considered.

Catalina shrugged. "Yeah, well, they loved each other regardless." She smiled at Fran, Charlie, and Louie. "I'm glad you three got to enjoy the spoils of Elysium. Tartarus, and especially Nyx's bedroom, is nothing to mess around with."

"What was it like?" Fran turned to face Milly, her eyes lighting up. "Did you guys have to fight Nyx?" Just then, she covered her mouth with her hands and looked nervously at Charon. He didn't seem to mind that they were talking about his mother, though. Perhaps he felt the same way towards her as Thanatos did, or perhaps he was simply indifferent. That wouldn't have surprised Milly, as eerie and ominous as Charon could be, he seemed to care about only one thing: getting paid.

Milly recounted to Fran, Charlie, Louie, Faramund, and Mirabel how they'd taken Nyx's most prized possession – how they'd snuck into her bedroom while she was sleeping, and how Thanatos had helped them, too. She asked Ashley to open the music box and show everyone the agate, which she happily did, – only for a horrible, spine-chilling noise to ring out and reverberate across the River Styx. Louie jumped at the sudden noise, burying his head between his paws. He was still easily startled by loud noises, ever since a balloon had burst at one of the children's parties.

"Bloody hell!" Harry exclaimed, clapping his hands over his ears. "What are you doing? Close that wretched thing already!"

Ashley quickly closed the music box, but not before Milly caught a glimpse of the beautiful, purple agate inside and thought it might have been a good idea to check it was still there before leaving. They had only just escaped in time. Thanatos had done right by them. She smiled broadly. The God of Death was an honest man. A few minutes later, they reached the dock near the entrance of the Underworld. Catalina paid Charon a few more gold coins and stepped out of the boat. The rest of the group followed suit, Ashley tucking the small music box into the sleeve of her tunic. "We did it," she said to Milly, grinning.

Milly grinned back. "We did it," she repeated. All they had to do now was make their way back to Alexandria. Catalina, Faramund, Wolfstan, and Mirabel claimed to know where Alexander the Great's tomb was. Their task now would be using the agate's magic to get inside.

Their journey back to Alexandria didn't take nearly as long as their journey to the Underworld. Fran, Charlie, and Louie seemed well-fed and well-rested after their time in Elysium, and Milly and her friends walked with a renewed energy. They had done it. The feeling of accomplishment continued to resonate in Milly's mind as they made their way towards the ancient city. Ashley had managed to take Nyx's agate out of the music box, but not without another "bloody hell!" from Harry and a howl from Louie. The noise seemed to bother Harry so much that he snatched the music box from Ashley and tossed it into the bushes.

"Oh, Harry," Milly said, as Ashley handed the agate to her. She could feel it radiating some sort of strange energy in her palm. "Honestly. Was that really necessary? This is something magical and otherworldly, all right."

Harry shrugged. "Hey, if anything, getting rid of that horrible music box will throw Nyx off our scent... you know, assuming she's following us."

Milly arched an eyebrow, craning her neck to look behind them. She didn't see anything. "I don't think she is," she said.

"Nyx can't follow us here," Catalina told them. "She can't leave the Underworld..." Then, in almost a whisper, she added, "I think."

"You think?" Lucy piped up. "Great. We'd better hurry up and raid Alexander's tomb. It seems like we're on borrowed time."

"What if we returned the agate to Nyx after we're done using it?" Fran asked. Louie barked in agreement, wagging his tail. "She can't be mad at us if we give it back, right?"

Catalina looked at her as if she were completely out of her mind. "We cannot confront Nyx," she said. "It's not safe. Lucy's right. We need to hurry if we're going to succeed in raiding the tomb of Alexander." Milly gave Fran an apologetic look. She liked the idea of returning the agate to Nyx, that way, Nyx wouldn't hold a grudge against them. Would she? She wasn't even sure whether Nyx had seen their faces. She was a little worried she might be able to get information out of Thanatos. Despite the fact they'd retrieved the joy that had been stolen from him, he was still under Nyx's thumb. She was his mother, after all. She tried to push the thought aside and focused on what they would do when they reached the entrance of Alexander's tomb instead.

"Okay..." Milly said, clearing her throat and slipping the agate into her pocket. "So, how are we going to use the agate to get into Alexander's tomb? Are we supposed to do a ritual or say some sort of incantation, or, we'll figure that out when we get there," Faramund said, lazily stretching his arms above his head. "In the meantime, maybe we can find something to eat?"

Wolfstan laughed. "You're always thinking about your stomach, aren't you, just like Louie? It's not a bad idea, though. There's a small amount of meat and bread left over if you lot would like a quick bite to eat before we break into Alexander's tomb. Ha!" He let out a boisterous laugh. "It feels funny saying that, doesn't it? King Jason is going to be so proud of us.

Just imagine the riches that lie within that tomb!" The others agreed, and a few minutes later, they sat down on a patch of grass to eat and watch the sunset over the horizon. Louie chewed on a couple of Louie chewies and drank water from Milly's outstretched hand.

"This is perfect," Catalina said with her mouth full of meat. "We shouldn't have any trouble sneaking into Alexander's tomb under the cover of night." Milly nodded and chatted with the others as the sky grew dim. She wondered what was in store for them next. What or who could be lurking in the depths of Alexander's tomb? Only time will tell.

A few hours later, they found themselves following Catalina through Alexandria, a city transformed under the night sky. Unlike the bustling daytime, it was now quiet and peaceful. The merchants had packed up their stalls, and the only figures visible were a handful of villagers bringing in their dry laundry and guards patrolling in front of Alexander's castle. "Ah, yes," Faramund said, wringing his hands. "I suppose we'll have to deal with the guards."

"Say no more," Wolfstan replied, casting a furtive glance around to ensure no one was observing before notching a sleep arrow on his bow. He shot the arrow with precision, striking one guard squarely in the shoulder blade. The guard instantly collapsed, crumpling to the ground in a deep slumber. Another guard, noticing the commotion, rushed over only to, find himself swiftly rendered unconscious by Wolfstan's expert aim. "I can handle the remaining guards if needed," he said, "but we should be able to sneak around the castle and make our way to the courtyard. That's where the entrance to Alexander's tomb is located."

"Right," Catalina agreed, gesturing for Milly, Wolfstan, and the others to follow her. "Let's go!" With Fran, Charlie, and Louie trailing behind, Milly, Ashley, Harry, and Lucy followed Catalina as they crept along the side of the vast castle. She barely had time to take in the chaotic aftermath of the raided courtyard, with pillars lying on their sides and debris scattered, everywhere when Mirabel interrupted her thoughts by pointing at a nondescript spot on the ground.

"There," she said. "There's a small trapdoor, of sorts, buried in the dirt. We just need to dig it up." Louie stepped up eagerly, as if this job had been made for him, and Milly suspected it had, given his knack for digging. He sniffed at the spot Mirabel had indicated moments before and began to kick up the dirt with his paws. It wasn't long before he unearthed exactly what Mirabel, had mentioned a small trapdoor that, to Milly's astonishment, was made of wood.

"Don't let him touch it!" Mirabel exclaimed urgently. "It has a spell on it that burns anyone who makes contact!"

Milly quickly seized Louie by the collar and pulled him away from the wooden door. She praised him with a hug around the neck. "Good boy," she said. "You did a fantastic job, Louie." The dog jumped up, planting a big kiss on her cheek, sensing he'd done well. After giving him a final pat on the head, Milly turned to Mirabel. "Okay... now what?"

Mirabel glanced at Catalina. "Uh... you read Agnes's tome, right? Did it mention how to activate Nyx's agate?"

Catalina nodded. "Yes, it did," she replied. "It stated that Nyx's agate is, likely, the key to unlocking Alexander's tomb, but it requires a specific activation method. Unfortunately, the tome was rather vague on the details."

Impatience welling up inside her, Milly pulled the agate from her pocket and placed it on the wooden trapdoor. She held her breath, eagerly awaiting a reaction. However, after a few minutes of nothing happening, her heart sank. They had come so far and faced numerous challenges, only to be met with another. But as she surveyed her friends' faces, she knew they wouldn't give up easily. "Perhaps we just need to try something," she suggested. "Like... saying a magic word."

Fran's eyes brightened with excitement. "Or maybe we need to use a piece of Athena's Shawl!" she exclaimed, pulling out a fragment she had retrieved from her backpack. "I brought it along so we could use it to find our way home. Maybe it's connected somehow!"

Catalina looked sceptical for a moment but then smiled and shrugged. "It's worth a try," she said. "Place the shawl over Nyx's agate and see what happens."

Fran nodded and, with shaky hands, placed the fragment of Athena's Shawl over the agate. Initially, nothing transpired. Then, to their astonishment, the agate began to emit a glow. With a soft click, the wooden trapdoor slid open, revealing a dark passageway that descended into the depths of Alexander's tomb.

"Wow," Harry remarked, sounding sceptical. "That... worked."

Milly swiftly snatched the agate and the piece of Athena's Shawl, stowing them away in her pocket. "Yes," she said, "it must be the moonlight shining through the Shawl that did it. Goodness, there remains so much we don't understand about this artefact!"

"Great job, Fran!" Catalina exclaimed, nearly bouncing with joy. "Let's not waste another minute. Treasures beyond our wildest dreams await us below!"

As the group stepped into Alexander's tomb, they found themselves traversing a narrow hallway that stretched into the darkness. They moved in single file, with Catalina leading the way and Fran cradling Louie at the rear. Milly followed closely behind Harry, who seemed to be battling his own anxieties as they made their way through the constricted passage. That's right, Milly thought to herself. Harry's claustrophobic. Reaching forward, she grasped his hand and squeezed it. Just as she was about to release it, Harry entwined his fingers with hers. "Don't let go," he said. "It helps." Milly couldn't suppress a broad grin.

The walls of Alexander's tomb were composed of smooth, cold stone, with surfaces etched in the same Persian symbols Milly had studied in her history class. The air felt thick and, stale, filled with the scent of dust and decay. As they walked, the echoes of their footsteps reverberated against the stone floor. In the distance, Milly thought she heard something else, ominous laughter followed by, moans but quickly dismissed it. My imagination must be playing tricks on me, she reasoned.

After several minutes, they arrived at a door at the end of the passageway. Milly's heart raced as they approached. Withheld breaths, the group pushed open the door and stepped into the room beyond. What greeted them was awe-inspiring. The chamber was vast and cavernous, with faded murals adorning its walls, depicting the legendary feats of Alexander the Great. Scattered throughout the chamber were several unlit torches positioned strategically in various corners of the room. Huh... Milly mused. This doesn't look too bad... until her gaze landed on the creatures hovering menacingly above them, enormous birds with sharp talons and the heads of human women.

"Harpies!" Mirabel cried, unsheathing her sword. "Quick, Wolfstan! Take them out with your sleep arrows!" However, Wolfstan lay fast asleep on the floor, along with Faramund and Harry. "Oh, great," Mirabel said, throwing her hands up in frustration. She knelt down to slap Wolfstan and Faramund gently on their faces, but it proved fruitless. "Hey! Wake up!"

"What happened?" Ashley asked, ducking to avoid one of the harpies swooping towards her. "These things are terrifying!"

"Harpies can put men to sleep," Mirabel replied, standing up again. "Is Charlie okay?"

"I'm fine!" Charlie yelled, using his body to shield Louie from the harpies, who was clearly frightened. "I guess it didn't affect me because I'm just a kid!"

"Good," Mirabel said, swinging her sword at one of the harpies. "Catalina! Milly! Ashley! Lucy! Let's fight!"

Catalina sprang into action, her throwing knives flashing through the air as she struck down several harpies with deadly precision. Joining her, Milly, Ashley, and Lucy leapt into the fray, their weapons ringing against those of the harpies as they fought to defend themselves. Charlie crouched next to Harry's sleeping form and seized his bow and quiver of arrows. Although the bow was comically large for him, he surprised Milly by successfully bringing down one of the slower harpies flying too high for their close-combat weapons to reach. "Did you see that, Milly?" he yelled. "Did you see?"

"I saw! Great job, Charlie!" Milly shouted over the chaos. She scanned the room for Louie, who was valiantly confronting one of the harpies, , baring his teeth and hurling himself at it until it retreated into the centre of the room. Charlie, now full of confidence, took another shot at the harpy, finally bringing it down, . With all the harpies either defeated or, incapacitated, an eerie silence enveloped the chamber once more.

Fran, who had been cowering behind her shield, dashed over to where Wolfstan, Faramund, and Harry lay sleeping. "Hello?" she nudged Harry with her foot. "Wake up already!"

Gradually, they blinked awake and pushed themselves up from the floor. "Sorry about that," Harry said, shaking the remnants of sleep from his mind. "What happened?"

"Bloody harpies," Wolfstan grumbled, rubbing his eyes. "That's a dirty trick."

"We dealt with them," Catalina assured. "But now, the question is: what do we do next?"

Milly and the others surveyed the chamber once more. Something about the unlit torches nagged at her, yet she couldn't quite grasp what it was. There was another door at the far end of the chamber, but it was obstructed by metal bars. "How are we going to get past that door?" she asked.

"Hmm..." Charlie appeared deep in thought. "I think I remember something. There was a puzzle like this in the Legend of Zelda game I was playing the other day."

"Who's Zelda?" Wolfstan inquired.

Covering her mouth to stifle a laugh, Charlie replied, "We need to light all of the torches at the same time. Do you have fire arrows, Wolfstan?"

"I do," Wolfstan said, deftly notching one onto his bow. "But it's nearly impossible to light them all at once; they're too spread out."

"I don't think they have to be lit at the same time," Ashley suggested. "They just need to stay lit, which means you'll have to be quick."

Wolfstan shrugged. "I'll give it a try." With extraordinary accuracy, he shot his fire arrows at each of the torches. It happened so fast that Milly could hardly believe her eyes. When all the torches flared to life, the metal bars over the door lifted. "Oh, hey! That worked! Make a break for that door! I don't think we have much time!"

The group sprinted for the door, and, just in the nick of time, they slipped through, the bars clanging down just inches behind Louie's tail. The room they entered was small and oddly empty. Hearing laughter followed by moaning again, , Milly felt an undeniable urge to confront it; the source of those noises was much closer this time. "I'm... not the only one who can hear that, right?" she asked her friends.

"I hear it too," Fran said, clutching Milly's elbow tightly.

"Yep," Catalina confirmed. "I've no idea what it is. Let's hope we won't have to find out."

As they cautiously explored the room, the source of the laughter and moaning revealed itself. In a dark corner, they discovered a small prison cell, its iron bars rusted and worn with age. Inside sat none other than Deimos Asgard, Milly's nemesis, his eyes wild with madness as he hugged his knees and laughed maniacally. Milly's heart raced at the sight of him. She had thought she'd seen the last of Deimos after her previous encounter, when she and her siblings rescued their mother from his clutches. And yet, here he was, locked away in Alexander's tomb.

"What... what are you doing here, Deimos?" Milly demanded, her voice quaking with anger. "How did you even get into Alexander's tomb?"

Deimos's laughter subsided, replaced by a chilling grin. "Ah, Milly," he said. "So delightful to see you again. As for how I arrived here... let's just say I have my ways. However, it appears I'm rather trapped at the moment. Perhaps we could set aside our differences? Will you help me escape?"

Milly clenched her fists, battling the fury rising within her. Deimos had always been one step ahead, consistently finding ways to create chaos in her life. But now, imprisoned, she possessed the upper hand. "You kidnapped my mother," she spat, her voice dripping with venom. "You put her through hell. Why on earth would I help you?"

Deimos's grin widened. "Oh, Milly dear," he purred. "I trust you're aware of the fabulous riches concealed within this tomb? If you assist me in escaping this cell, I can lead you to the very heart of Alexander's tomb. That's where his coffin lies... along with all his treasures."

Milly's eyes narrowed at his words. She knew better than to trust anything that escaped his lips, yet the promise of untold treasures piqued her interest. "And what makes you think I would trust you?" she retorted. "You've caused nothing but tumult every time we've crossed paths. Why should I believe you now?"

Deimos's grin faltered slightly, but his eyes sparkled with a conspiratorial intensity. "Because, dear Milly, we both desire the same outcome," he said. "We both seek the treasures of Alexander the Great. With my cunning and your skills, together we could unlock the secrets of this tomb."

Milly hesitated, torn between her urge for revenge against Deimos Asgard and her curiosity about the treasures hidden within the tomb. She glanced at her friends, who were watching the exchange with a mixture of apprehension and disbelief. Louie bared his teeth and emitted a series of growls, causing Deimos to pause for an instant.

Lucy stepped forward, carefully removing her Kirby pin from her hair. "Perhaps we should listen to him," she suggested. "If there's a chance we can uncover Alexander's riches while stopping Deimos at the same time, it might be worth the risk."

Milly frowned, fully aware that trusting Deimos was a dangerous gamble... but the temptation of Alexander's treasures loomed too heavily to ignore. After a moment of tense contemplation, she nodded reluctantly. "Fine," she said. "Go ahead and pick the lock, Lucy. But if you attempt anything treacherous, Deimos, I won't hesitate to shove you back into that cell myself."

Deimos's grin reappeared, his eyes gleaming with victory. "Agreed," he purred, his voice smooth as silk.

10

DEIMOS ASGARD

To Milly's surprise, Deimos Asgard remained true to his word. His apparent honesty, however, didn't deter Catalina from pressing the blunt side of her knife against his back, while Louie paced menacingly behind him as he guided them through the labyrinthine corridors of Alexander's tomb. He was surprisingly loquacious, which annoyed Milly to no end. She had no interest in hearing about how long he'd been trapped in that prison cell or that he had been subsisting on bugs to survive. She despised him and wanted nothing more than to part ways with him as swiftly as possible. Louie clearly shared her mistrust; he continued to growl at Deimos and nip at his ankles as they navigated the narrow corridors, his instincts on high alert.

Eventually, they arrived at an enormous door adorned with intricate Persian symbols and gold trim. There was no doubt this was the entrance to

Alexander's sarcophagus, where his untold riches were

concealed. Wolfstan attempted to push the door open, but, as expected, it didn't budge. Faramund, Mirabel, Catalina, and Harry stepped forward to assist, but their efforts were in vain. "This is as far as I managed to get," Deimos informed them, a hint of smugness in his voice. "Perhaps you can open the door, Milly. You're a descendant of Athena, aren't you?"

"Yeah..." Milly replied, recalling that the torn piece of Athena's Shawl was tucked away in the pocket of her tunic. "So, what?"

"Well... Alexander's tomb is protected by Athena. Perhaps she'll open the door for you," Deimos suggested, his tone almost mocking.

Milly glanced at her companions, still harbouring doubts about Deimos's intentions. Catalina nodded, her expression encouraging. "Give it a try, Milly," she urged.

Taking a deep breath, Milly moved toward the door, her heart pounding in her chest. To her surprise, Fran approached it alongside her, with, Louie and Charlie close behind. "Fran?" Milly said, placing her hand on the stone door, feeling its cool surface beneath her fingertips.

"Let's do this together," Fran replied, her voice steady and resolute. Louie barked in agreement, and Charlie stood back, filled with admiration for his sisters' bravery.

Slowly but surely, they managed to push open the hefty door, the sound echoing ominously in the stillness of the tomb. The group filtered into the room, which was, just as Milly had suspected, filled to the brim with gold coins, extravagant jewellery, and silver goblets that sparkled in the dim light. In the centre stood a large golden sarcophagus, its surface gleaming with an otherworldly glow. Alexander's resting place, she thought, her heart racing with disbelief. I can't believe it.

"This is incredible," Lucy exclaimed, dipping her hand into a pile of gold coins, her eyes wide with wonder. "There's more than enough here to pay off your dad's loan shark, Harry... we're all going to be rich!"

Fran and Charlie exchanged glances at the mention of the debt. "What debt? Was this trip about money?" Fran queried, her brow furrowing in confusion.

Deimos Asgard was already busy stuffing his pockets, the old scoundrel. Though Milly couldn't judge him too harshly; she was there to do the same.

Milly looked at her siblings and began to explain the 'small' deception, while Louie continued to growl and tug at Deimos's cloak, clearly unimpressed with the man's antics.

"You mean you lied to Mum about this whole adventure being about school stuff?" Fran asked incredulously, her eyes wide with disbelief. "How could you do that?"

Harry shifted uncomfortably; he hadn't anticipated their reaction. "Look, Fran, I promise this isn't solely about that. I... I mean, Harry is our friend, and we wouldn't want anything bad to happen to him, right?" Milly asserted, her voice firm.

"I'm glad we could help you, Harry. I hope this is a big help," Charlie added, his youthful optimism shining through.

Harry nodded silently, and the group awaited Fran's response, except for Deimos, who was still busily stuffing his cloak with gold.

"Thinking about it, it doesn't really matter, right?" Fran eventually said, her tone softening. "I'm sorry for trying to make a big deal out of it. Anything for you, Harry."

"Thank you. So, does that mean you won't tell Mum and Dad?" Milly asked, her heart racing with hope.

"My lips are sealed. This stays between us," Fran promised, her expression earnest.

"Cool," Lucy chimed in, her mood lifting slightly.

Just then, the chamber began to rumble ominously. A dreadful, anguished voice resonated throughout the tomb, sending shivers down Milly's spine. "WHERE... IS... MY... AGATE?"

"Is that...?" Mirabel paused while gathering jewellery into her travel bag, her eyes wide with fear.

"It's Nyx," Catalina declared, her voice filled with urgency. "I feared this would happen. We need to hurry. Grab what you can, and let's get out of here!"

Milly watched as Harry began to fill his school bag with fistfuls of golden coins. Lucy did the same, while Wolfstan and Faramund wasted no time filling their travel bags as well. Only Milly, Fran, Charlie, and Ashley hesitated to lay claim to the treasure. Milly still grappled with her moral qualms regarding the situation, while Fran and Charlie cowered in fear as Nyx's enormous footsteps approached, echoing ominously through the chamber.

Louie whined, tugging at the back of Milly's tunic as if urging her to hurry. She scooped him into her arms and signalled for Fran, Charlie, Harry, and the others to follow her. "Come on," she urged, "we don't have much time, ." But it was already too late. An enormous woman came crashing through the door, her flowing purple robes and long black hair swirling around her like a tempest.

"Nyx!" Milly shouted, adrenaline surging through her. She had to act fast. "Fran, give me your backpack. I need that picture of Mum and Dad." As Nyx advanced toward them, Fran rummaged through her bag and finally retrieved the photograph of their parents standing outside their house, smiling brightly.

Milly swiftly extracted Athena's Shawl from her pocket, causing Nyx's agate to slip from her grasp, shattering into a million pieces as it hit the ground.

"No!" Nyx screeched, rage filling her voice. "What have you done?"

"We need a light source," Milly stated, her mind racing with possibilities.

"Here, use one of my fire arrows," Wolfstan said, reaching into his quiver. The tip of the arrow ignited, granting Milly just enough illumination to work with.

"Everyone, join hands!" she instructed her friends. Fran and Charlie grasped her elbows, while Harry, Ashley, Lucy, and the four crusader knights linked hands behind them. Milly held a scrap of Athena's Shawl up to the flame, ensuring that the picture of her parents was projected onto it. "Come on, come on..." she urged, willing the shawl to perform its magic. "Ahhh! Let go of me, Deimos!" She felt the evil priest's hand wrap around her wrist; there was nothing she could do. The last sight before being lifted into the air and pulled through space and time was Nyx's claw-like hand reaching for her...

Then, with a plop, she landed in her bedroom, Louie safely nestled in her arms. Fran and Charlie tumbled down beside her, and the others followed soon after. Suddenly, her bedroom felt overcrowded, but she was relieved they had made it, that they had achieved their goal of raiding Alexander the Great's tomb. Still, a significant problem had accompanied them: Deimos Asgard.

It was strange to see him sprawled on the carpet next to her desk, looking around, in confusion, as were Catalina, Mirabel, Wolfstan, and Faramund. This was their first glimpse of the future. "Where... where am I?" Deimos exclaimed, his tone frantic. Then, , his eyes landed on Athena's Shawl in all its glory, draped before Milly's window. "Yes!" he cried. "I must have it!" He hoisted himself up, reaching out to touch it, but Catalina was quicker.

"Not so fast," she said, hurling one of her throwing knives at Deimos. She successfully pinned him against the wall, while Louie, , as brave as ever, , growled at him to assert dominance as he struggled and pushed him further into the wall.

"Let me go this instant!" Deimos demanded, just as Milly's parents burst into the room, their expressions a mix of bewilderment and concern.

"What's going on in here?" her father inquired, his voice filled with authority. "Who are you people?"

"Hi, Mr and Mrs Martin," Lucy said, waving at Milly's parents, her tone casual despite the chaos. "Apologies for the ruckus..."

Milly's mother looked alarmed, her eyes darting to Deimos Asgard. "What... what is that man doing here?" she asked, regarding him with apprehension. "Milly? Fran? Charlie? Are you okay?"

"We're okay, Mum," Fran assured her, her voice steady. "Deimos Asgard grabbed Milly's wrist while she was using Athena's Shawl to bring us back home."

"Well?" Their father appeared at a loss for words, his brow furrowing. "What are we supposed to do with him? I have an overwhelming urge to punch him in the face, but..."

"I'll take care of this," Harry said, rising from the floor and striding over to where Deimos was pinned. "I'm fed up with all the trouble you've caused for Milly and her family," he addressed the evil priest, his voice filled with determination. "We should never have let you out of that prison cell, but Milly showed you mercy." To Milly's astonishment, he hoisted Deimos over his shoulder with a grunt. "You're heavier than you look," he said, "but it's time you went back to where you belong." He ensured that "War of the Ages 2" continued to be projected onto Athena's Shawl, grasped Milly's hand, and promptly thrust Deimos Asgard through the portal before he could react. Milly thought she heard him scream: "This isn't over! I will acquire Athena's Shawl one day!" but it could have been her imagination.

Harry quickly removed the shawl from the window and handed it to Milly. "Perhaps you should store this somewhere a bit safer?" he suggested, his tone serious. "Just a thought."

Milly's heart raced once again. It felt as if everyone else in the room had , vanished, leaving just her and Harry. Without thinking, she grasped his face and kissed him swiftly on the lips. Coming back to her senses a moment too late, she jumped away, her cheeks burning with embarrassment. "Er... sorry," she stammered, her heart pounding. "Thank you for, uh... dealing with him."

Harry's face turned crimson, a shy grin spreading across his features. "Hey... there's no need to apologise," he replied, his voice warm and reassuring.

"Milly..." John Martin cleared his throat, his expression a mix of confusion and concern. "What was that all about?"

"Milly has a boyfriend!" Fran sang teasingly, her eyes sparkling with mischief.

"Shut up. No, I don't," Milly retorted, though she couldn't help but smile at the playful banter.

A few minutes later, she was bidding farewell to Catalina, Mirabel, Faramund, and Wolfstan once again. "Thank you for everything," she said earnestly, her heart swelling with gratitude. "You four are truly my heroes."

"Aw," Catalina replied, blushing slightly. "You and Louie are our heroes too. We're already eagerly anticipating our next adventure together. Now, uh... if you could set up Athena's Shawl again so we can go home..."

"Right," Milly said, taping the shawl back into its usual position in the window. Once everyone had exchanged their goodbyes, the crusader knights slipped into Athena's Shawl once more, aided by Milly and Fran. "Until next time," Milly said, tears welling in her eyes. She then turned to her parents, who still appeared somewhat perplexed. "Hi," she greeted, a bit more timidly than before.

"Hi, yourself," her mother chuckled lightly, her expression softening. "So... I take it you've collected all the information you need for your history report?"

"Oh, right... that," Milly stammered, her mind racing. "Uh... yep!" She was too exhausted to explain everything right now. She would do so soon enough.

Ashley and Lucy departed for dinner, and Milly found herself standing on the front porch with Harry. So much had happened, and yet she hadn't uncovered her special powers, or perhaps she had caught a glimpse of them when wielding the sword, . Charlie hadn't discovered his either. Fran, it seemed, could communicate with animals but hadn't yet harnessed that ability fully. Maybe their mother had been right; perhaps they were still too young. They would just have to wait. She glanced at Harry, who couldn't seem to stop grinning. "So..." he said, breaking the silence, "you kissed me."

"Whatever," Milly replied, suppressing a grin. "You kissed me back... and you'd better not tell anyone. Ashley and Lucy are already going to give me grief about it at school tomorrow."

"I won't," he said, patting his book bag. "You helped me raid Alexander's tomb, after all. I'm not sure how I'll ever repay you."

She gazed into his eyes, allowing herself, for once, to embrace her true feelings. "Kiss me again, and we'll call it even," she said, as Louie, sensing the impending moment, hid his head between his paws, seemingly oblivious to the tension in the air.

www.ingramcontent.com/pod-product-compliance
Lightning Source LLC
Chambersburg PA
CBHW040529170726
48295CB00012B/393